G.k. Hall Romance

W9-CEE-469

MEN ARE SUCH FOOLS!

MEN ARE
SUCH FOOLS!

FAITH BALDWIN

G.K. Hall & Co. • Chivers Press
Waterville, Maine USA   Bath, England

This Large Print edition is published by G.K. Hall & Co., USA
and by Chivers Press, England.

Published in 2002 in the U.S. by arrangement with
Harold Ober Associates, Inc.

Published in 2002 in the U.K. by arrangement with
the author's estate.

U.S.   Hardcover   0-7838-9738-3 (Romance Series Edition)
U.K.   Hardcover   0-7540-4801-2 (Chivers Large Print)

The text of this Large Print edition is unabridged.
Other aspects of the book may vary from the original edition.

Set in 16 pt. Plantin by Minnie B. Raven.

Printed in the United States on permanent paper.

British Library Cataloguing-in-Publication Data available

Library of Congress Cataloging-in-Publication Data

Baldwin, Faith, 1893–
     Men are such fools! / Faith Baldwin.
        p. cm.
     ISBN 0-7838-9738-3 (lg. print : hc : alk. paper)
     1. Women executives — Fiction.   2. Married women — Fiction.
     3. Large type books.   I. Title.
PS3505.U97 M46 2002
813'.52—dc21   2001051836

To GRAEME LORIMER in deep appreciation

List of Chapters

Chapter One:

YOUNG WOMAN ON HER WAY

The stocky young man with the brown eyes and the red, unruly hair looked across the table at the Moon of His Delight. He glared at her. And the moon suffered an instant, dramatic eclipse.

"But, Jimmy —" she said plaintively.

She had a low voice and, at the moment, a high color. She was divinely fair, fashionably slender, and just tall enough. She was twenty-two years old and her name was Lina Lawrence. A pretty name, alliterative. Yet it was relative to her surname that they had been quarreling for the last two hours.

The Italian table d'hôte was crowded. Smoke rose to the low ceiling, blue and clinging, and partially obscured the incredible murals of impossibly blue harbors, unlikely green vineyards, and cow-eyed peasants making love in something which might have been moonlight. Where the walls were cracked the murals looked like impressionistic paintings of minor earthquakes. In the close confines of the room the clatter of thick china and thin silver was exciting or irritating, according to your mood.

What air there was was redolent, over the smoke, with oil, meat sauce, garlic. In the far corner Antonio's stellar attraction, a tubercular gentleman with sideburns and a mandolin, was

7

making the night, if not hideous, at least vocal, with tenor advertising of the charms of Santa Lucia.

Jimmy and Lina appeared to have lost the full use of several of their senses. They did not smell the garlic, they did not hear the thin, erratic tenor rising above the sound and fury of the dishes, and they had eyes for none save themselves.

Their waiter hovered in the distant background and beamed upon them paternally. A slightly soiled apron covered a large stomach, and a waistcoat, greening at the edges, hid a heart of gold; a heart which despite his enormous wife and six children, still reacted to Young Love. And this Jimmy and Lina represented. He knew them well. They had been coming to Antonio's for the past eight months. With moist black eyes he had observed the progress of their romance. Tonight it was patent to him that all was not as it should be, yet he did not feel discouraged. A little quarrel now and then was like a clove of garlic — it stimulated the appetite.

"I'm fed up with waiting," said Jimmy gloomily.

Lina put her hand on the table. She did so carelessly, as it were, without malice aforethought. Instantly the hand of Mr. Hall went out and covered it. They sat there, for a moment, looking at each other, lost, mindless, forgetful of the world. And the waiter sighed, remembering other days, and his Rosa, slim as this blond young woman was slim, but with night-dark hair, her mouth red as a rose, sweet as grapes . . .

"I do love you, Jimmy," said Lina, low.

After a moment he squared his shoulders and lifted one eyebrow at her. "But you won't marry me," he said.

"You know I will — whenever you say — but only if I can keep on working. Jimmy, we've been over this a hundred times —"

"A thousand!"

"Probably. It's only sensible. We're making practically the same money. We can more than get along on seventy a week. We can't, on thirty-odd — and that's flat."

He said stubbornly, "Lina, I want a home —"

Lina lifted her shoulders in exasperation. She said, "You'd *have* a home, you idiot. Would it make it more of a home if I were in it all day instead of coming back to it at night?"

"Sure it would," said Jimmy.

"Darling, you're impossible!" Lina drew her hand from under his warm, possessive touch, and sat back. She wore the funniest little hat, flaring back from her wide, white forehead. Her hair curled beneath it and her eyes were dark gray. She said shortly, "You haven't any conception of what living on thirty a week — two people, that is — would mean. I have. I've seen plenty . . . All I want. Not for me. And besides, I like my job. It has a future. I haven't slaved to

9

get this far and —"

"Sometimes," he said glumly, "I think you're nuts."

Lina looked at the watch strapped on her slender wrist. She said, "It's almost ten. We've been here nearly four hours — let's go —"

Jimmy signaled for his check. Two seven-course dinners, eighty-five cents. Tip. When the waiter had gone for change he stated, "I'll see you tomorrow night."

"No," replied Lina casually, "you won't. I'm going out with Bill Ryder."

"Ryder!" repeated Jimmy incredulously.

"You heard me," she said indifferently.

Her eyes were sometimes the color of doves, sometimes the color of rain and sometimes the color of steel. They were steel gray now and steel hard. The waiter rolled back with the change and Jimmy waved it away. It was more than usual. The waiter murmured blessings and departed. Lina reproached, "You gave him too much!"

"Skip it," said Jimmy. "I thought we'd thrashed out this Ryder business. Settled it. Three months ago you said you wouldn't let him date you. You promised."

"I know," she admitted, "and I kept it. But, Jimmy, we're getting nowhere. We see each other almost every evening. We bicker and quarrel and argue. It wears me out, I tell you. I can't *stand* it," she said urgently. "I've got to have a little fun, haven't I, some relaxation? So — I'm going out with Bill Ryder. Take it and like it. Or," she added, "leave it. I'm getting to the place where I just don't care."

She rose and he followed her move, mechanically. The waiter sprang forward to help them with their wraps. Presently they were out in the soft spring night, vocal with children and poisonous with carbon monoxide gas.

They walked along in silence. Jimmy's hands were deep in his pockets. When they reached the near-by building in which Lina shared a flat with another girl, she said, "Nan's in — tonight — want to come up?"

"No," said Jimmy. He took her by the shoulders, careless of possible onlookers. He demanded, "Lina, you're not serious about — Ryder?"

"I'm not," said Lina, "and he isn't serious about me. But we have good times together."

It was utterly final. He said, a little wildly, "Lina, you don't, you *can't* love me. If you did, you'd take your chances with me. I won't be a wagon salesman forever — with any luck there'll be a district salesmanship some day. I — I can't be content with these snatches of you."

She said wearily, "Let's not begin that again."

Turning, she went up the steps. Jimmy followed her, caught her in the gloom of the doorway, took her in his arms and kissed her, very adequately. For a moment she yielded, softening, clinging to him, while incurious people passed on the street below and a misty moon hung over the city and Washington Square was a fantasy of light and shadow.

But her surrender was brief. She detached herself, murmured something and went on in and up the echoing, ramshackle stairs. She was depressed, exasperated as she always was when she set her will, vainly, against Jimmy's. He was so stubborn, she thought angrily. She believed her attitude toward their problem eminently sensible and right, and felt that her power to resist his arguments was a proof of the strength of her character.

She was suddenly too tired to find her latchkey. She rapped on the door panel and Nancy said lazily, "Come on in, it's open."

Nancy, lying on the studio divan, which was also her bed, looked up and grinned. She was a plump girl, somewhat older than her friend, with mouse-brown hair, pink cheeks, and bright blue eyes. She wore a cotton kimono which had seen better days, her hair was in metal curlers, and she was reading a motion-picture magazine. A small radio was dutifully emitting the curious sounds normal to a crooner.

"You look dead," said Nancy sympathetically, and Lina nodded dully.

"Sit down," Nancy suggested, "and take the weight off your feet." She reached out and snapped off the radio. "I'm going sour on that guy," she announced. "But I heard a new baritone tonight — Boy, he's got sumpin'!"

12

Lina, putting her things away, wasn't listening. She was accustomed to Nancy's enthusiasms. Nancy read newspapers and magazines solely to keep herself informed upon the latest contracts, heart interests, divorces, tribulations, and triumphs of her various screen and radio idols. She was engagingly fickle. You never knew whose autographed photograph you'd find next, thumbtacked, over her dresser. She stood patiently in line at cinema palaces and fought her way in, to gaze spellbound at the current hero of her maiden dreams. For perhaps three months he would be top man. Then she wearied, and he was replaced.

She was a typist in the Americo organization. Her job was routine work for the clever and efficient secretary of one of the executives. Nancy, during her first weeks with Americo, had been in love with that executive in a tentative and resigned way, as if she felt that it was expected of her. It is doubtful if that gentleman ever knew she existed. But her brief passion gave her a certain prestige in her own eyes. Almost any girl could be in love with her boss, but it took one of imagination to be in love with her boss's boss, didn't it?

She was, however, agreeably engaged to a young man who sold insurance and whose claim upon her affections in no way interfered with, or encroached upon, her outside emotional outlets.

"How's Jimmy?"

"He's all right —" Lina sat down in a deep shabby chair and took off her shoes. She wriggled her slender toes and looked anxiously at a caught silk thread. "I believe," she said, "I'm going to have a run. Darn these stockings, anyway."

She lay back and closed her eyes. Nancy looked across at her with the generous and unusual admiration of a plain girl for a very pretty one. The one big room, shabby and crowded, had a pleasant, lived-in air. The worn rugs had seen better days and the cheap curtains were bright and gay. The two divans were heaped with cushions and spread with India print covers. There were pictures on the walls, and several pieces of really good furniture that had come to Lina from her mother's things.

"Tad didn't call up tonight?" Lina asked presently.

"Nope," said Nancy and plied industriously in a candy box for a nougat, "he had a lead — someone knew someone who knew someone who was sure to buy a one-hundred-thousand annuity if approached the right way. So he's out getting letters of introduction. Have a good time?"

"All right."

"You two been fighting again?" asked Nancy. She was always too indolent to be anything save direct.

"Not exactly."

"Better get it off your chest. Come on, tell Mama."

"Same old thing," said Lina, and stifled a yawn. "Wants me to marry him and quit working."

"Might be a good bet at that," remarked Nancy reflectively.

Lina snapped upright. "You know how I feel —"

Nancy held up a warning hand. It was manicured, the nails were scarlet, and there was a smudge of chocolate on her forefinger. She said, "Sure. But wait till Tad brings home just a few more pounds of bacon. You won't catch me slaving my life away at America, getting battered to death in subways, and taking any more of Yelland's dry ice: 'just a little more accuracy, Miss Robinson . . .' 'Do you think, Miss Robinson, that if you concentrated very hard to the temporary exclusion of your outside interests you could grasp what I am trying to tell you?' "

Nancy's mimicry of Mrs. Yelland's cultured and refrigerated tones was astonishingly good. It always made Lina laugh. She said, after a moment, "That's all very well for you, Nancy, you don't want to work — I mean, it's only marking time with you, a stopgap. But I like it. I — I want to go places! Jimmy hasn't any right to ask me to give it up —"

"Especially," suggested Nancy shrewdly, "when you think he hasn't anything better to offer?"

Lina didn't like her tone, particularly. She looked up quickly and her eyes darkened, the

15

pupils big and black. She said, "That's just about it," challengingly.

"But you love him," Nancy reminded her.

Lina rose from her chair and walked across the room to her cupboard. She took out robe, slippers, and nightgown, and her reply came, slightly muffled, to the older girl. "Of course," she admitted; "what has that to do with it?"

"Oh, nothing," answered Nancy, when Lina reappeared. "That is, from your point of view. I guess I must be mid-Victorian or something. I had a dim idea it made a difference."

Lina blazed at her. She cried furiously, "You've got me all wrong if you believe I'm not in love with Jimmy. I am. I — I'm *crazy* about him —" Her voice broke arid the gray eyes were full of tears. The high color which always rose under emotion was flooding upward from her slender throat. "Just because I'm not senti-mental — just because I haven't that woman's-place-is-in-the-home idea! I'm a lot more likely to stay in love with Jimmy and he's a lot more likely to stay in love with me if we don't begin our married life under the usual handicaps."

"Such as — ?" murmured Nancy, frightened, yet fascinated. It wasn't the first time she'd begun this argument with Lina. But it was the first time she'd seen her so aroused. Perhaps, thought Nancy erroneously, she isn't quite as sure, perhaps she's slipping.

"Poverty," replied Lina, "genteel style. Walk-ups and dirty dishes and — and — babies —

16

and rent due and doctor's bills to meet, and neither time nor money nor energy to try to keep yourself looking halfway human. Setting your own wave —"

Nancy put her hand to her head and Lina, stamping a small foot, cried, "Idiot! I didn't mean you — I meant — oh, letting yourself go, getting lax and careless, quarreling because you're both tired and worried . . ." She broke off and laughed a little shakily. "Sorry," she apologized briefly.

She went without further word into the dark and leprous bathroom with its vocal plumbing, its half-size tub and the washbasin that rocked if you leaned against it. Nancy settled back on the couch and picked up her magazine and tried to immerse herself in the story of a female star who, addressing the working girl, said firmly that it was ridiculous to expend more than five thousand a year on your clothes. On five thousand any girl could be smartly dressed.

"You're telling me!" murmured Nancy to the photograph of the star, smartly caparisoned in several tons of Russian sable and chinchilla.

The downstairs phone rang shrilly and presently footsteps plodded up a flight or two and the voice of their landlord announced a call for Lina. Nancy shouted back and called to Lina, "Phone for you!"

"I'll be right there," said Lina, appearing at once, scrubbed, chastened, in robe and slippers. She went hurriedly away from the room and Nancy, cocking an eyebrow, resumed her reading. Presently Lina returned. She was smiling.

"Jimmy, I presume," deduced Nancy, yawning; "you look like the w.k. cat."

"It was Bill Ryder," Lina told her.

Nancy was open-mouthed. "But, I thought —"

"Yes, I know," said Lina gayly. "I thought so too. We were both wrong. I'm going out with him tomorrow night. I told Jimmy so. I left a message for Bill at his hotel this noon. He's been out on the road. Well, he's back. Dinner, show, night club. Thank the Lord my periwinkle crepe's been pressed. The silver slippers are tarnished, but not too much." She shed robe and slippers, and deftly adjusted her slim weight to the sagging springs of her bed-divan. After a moment she asked, "May I wear your velvet wrap with the lapin?"

Nancy said, "Sure. Why describe it? It's all I own. Look here, Lina, you promised Jimmy — You said yourself you were getting tired of Bill Ryder. After all, he did make a few passes —"

Lina sat up. Her fair hair curled about her lovely, small face and her eyes were as hard as her skin was soft. She said angrily, "I can manage Bill. He thinks he's the playboy of the world. He believes certain gestures are expected of him, so he makes 'em. When nothing further happens I think he's relieved. He makes plenty of money; he knows how to have a good time."

18

Nancy said, bewildered, "You told me your-self you were glad to break with him. You said it came too high. Evening clothes, new slippers, and the dry-cleaning bills. You said he bored you."

"Don't be dumb," ordered Lina sharply. "Certainly it's expensive and of course he bores me. But I'm fed to the teeth with this silly atti-tude on Jimmy's part. I've used every argu-ment. I've tried to reason with him and he can't see things my way. All right, I'll try Bill as an argument."

Nancy commented slowly, "Just the same, it isn't fair to Jimmy."

Lina flung back her head and laughed. "Nancy, you're wonderful. Fair to Jimmy! How about being fair to me for a while? You can't be honest with men; it doesn't pay. They've got all the breaks. They do as they please, they're not handicapped as we are. We have to fight for every inch of ground. There's only one way to do it. Never let them be sure of you, never let them take you for granted. If you can't get what you want one way, you can get it another. Here's an example. I'd still be a typist if I hadn't gone out with Sam Perkins and learned something about the advertising department, outside of typing. Or if I hadn't called myself to Mr. Welles's attention and begged to try my hand on those promotion booklets for bill stuffers. Well, what happened? Last week I was put in charge of that work, with a five-dollar raise."

"Meantime," said Nancy, "you'd given Sam the air."

"Oh," said Lina, "long ago. As soon as I knew I didn't need him — He was a laugh. But he knew his job. I wanted to know it too. Nancy, don't look as if I'd hit you with a brick. If you don't use men, they'll use you. You have to use them to get ahead. You can't get along on your own. After Father deserted us and we went to live with relatives I saw my mother kicked around, plenty, with every morsel she ate shoved down her throat as charity. After she died it might have been the same for me, living with this aunt and that, expected to mind the squalling babies. But I'm not like my mother. I made myself useful in a lot of ways to Uncle Ned, so, after he saw me through high school, he financed my business course here. And I got my job with Americo. I see why Aunt Nell married him, he's so soft — you can get anything out of him, if you go about it right. I did. It just meant listening to what he did in the war, and fetching his slippers and reading the newspaper aloud and going out hunting. Aunt Nell hates the look of a gun. I do too, but that didn't matter. So here I am. I have a good job, I'll get a better one. And Jimmy can't stop me. I'm going places. He's been too sure of me, for a long time."

Nancy asked curiously, "You think that Bill Ryder . . . ?"

"I don't think," said Lina, "I know. You

20

watch Jimmy Hall come to time!" She snapped off the bedside light and lay down. After a moment she remarked drowsily, *"Men are such fools —"*

Chapter Two:

PROGRESS —
IN LOVE AND IN BUSINESS

After leaving Lina, Jimmy walked up to a motion-picture house on Eighth Street. He was disinclined to return to the noisy, crowded flat he shared with four other men. Three of them were employed by public utilities and the fourth was Kit Fawcett, a detail salesman with Americo. Only Americo employees didn't say "detail salesman," they said, "missionary," and let it go at that.

Kit wouldn't be home yet. The others might be in, reading, radio going full blast, coats and shoes off, room full of smoke. They were all right, but he didn't want to go back yet and take the usual ribbing. They all knew about Lina, and that she was holding out on him because of her job. They had settled notions about women and jobs. Probably, he thought, crossing the street against the light, to the consternation of a truck driver, a lady from Dubuque, and a wild-eyed cop, because none of them was in love with a girl who wanted to keep on working after marriage.

It was, he thought, trying to find excuses for her, quite natural that she couldn't see things his way. She'd had no home since babyhood. She didn't have memories, actual roots. He'd had a home and all that went with it, until his parents' automobile accident. He had been seventeen then. Those seventeen years were important — they had molded him.

He went into the motion-picture house, sat in the back row and watched the superb outlines of Miss Joan Crawford move across the screen. But he wasn't thinking of Miss Crawford. He was thinking of Lina. She hadn't been serious about Bill Ryder. She couldn't be. She knew what he thought of Ryder. He was — no good. A lightweight. She couldn't mean that she'd start seeing him again. Why would she want to? — he didn't mean anything to her. Surely not because he could browbeat head waiters, order champagne, and make off-color wisecracks during the floor show!

Presently he convinced himself that Lina had not meant it; she was sore at him; she was tired. Tomorrow night he'd see her. They'd go to Antonio's again, or to Millie's, where they could dance, or uptown to Schrafft's for the ice-cream cake she loved. They'd make up again. They'd have a celebration as they had last week when she'd had her raise, and he'd pay the check again, instead of going fifty-fifty, as she always demanded. He smiled, thinking of her. "I'm not just doing it to be fair to you, Jimmy. I know lots of men whose money I'd as soon waste. But this is our money. And you overtip and order too much. You've got to save."

He remembered the first time he saw her, in the Americo lobby. It was thronged with people, hurrying home, but he'd seen only Lina. He remembered the turn of her head and the gray eyes filled with laughter and the fair hair curling about her sweetly shaped face. He remembered his moment of exultation when he saw she was with a girl whom he knew slightly. Boy, oh, boy, he'd told himself, this is a break for me!

He'd fallen in love with her then. There were no two ways about it.

When the picture had run its course he left the theater. Perhaps Kit would be back home by now, after his sortie into darkest Flatbush to see his girl. Jimmy, striding along, thought he must remember to tell Lina what Kit had told him this morning — about the woman complaining in the retail store about the new gadget for pouring Oceanic Salt. She didn't like it, it stuck, poured too much or not at all. Kit had been at the counter when she voiced her complaint to the grocer. She'd ruined a perfectly good mulligan stew, she reported indignantly, her husband had acquired such a thirst he'd gone out and got himself blind drunk at Kelly's! So he was home sick, half a week's wages spent and two days' work lost all because Oceanic Salt had a new container which wasn't worth the extra cent charged because of it. So she'd switch to another brand next time, thank you very kindly.

He'd tell Lina tomorrow. It had gone out of his head tonight. But tomorrow, at Millie's perhaps, with the orchestra going, he'd tell her and she'd laugh and narrow her eyes at him in the way she had. She wasn't like most girls, hating any mention of business. She liked it. She was sold on Americo.

Americo controlled a dozen or more packaged foods with nationally known names and trademarks, and was served by Jimmy in the capacity of a wagon salesman earning, with commissions, from thirty to thirty-five dollars a week.

It was an enormous business. So enormous that it was a minor miracle that it did not become top-heavy. Wagon salesmen, like Jimmy, were under the control of the sales department. There was a sales manager for each product and a district manager over each district for all products. Look beyond the district manager and you'd find an executive vice-president. And if you could manage to look beyond him you might glimpse faintly, so far away that he was practically legendary, a president over all operations.

Yes, it was a big outfit, the biggest and the best known of its kind in the United States. There were factories all over the country, each with its separate set-up and its tie-up in the executive offices in New York. There was the advertising department, which worked in conjunction with the outside advertising

25

agency which handled the accounts, and there were the chemical and biological laboratories with their separate yet dovetailed set-ups as well.

Reaching the apartment, Jimmy was himself again. Everything was going to be all right. Lina would see reason; she hadn't really intended going out with Bill Ryder; tomorrow was another day and a good one.

But when, the following evening, he presented himself at Lina's place, climbed the stairs whistling and knocked at the door, Nancy opened to him.

She looked, he saw, a little embarrassed at seeing him. "Where's Lina?" he asked, trying to look past her into the room.

"She's gone out, Jimmy."

"But —"

"She didn't expect you," Nancy assured him, repeating what Lina had told her to say and not liking it very much.

"That's crazy," said Jimmy hotly. "I told her I'd see her tonight."

"But," said Nancy, "she had a date with Bill Ryder. She said you knew she was going."

He felt like an idiot. Nancy's eyes were soft, pitying, and a tall figure moved up behind her, grinned at him, said, "Hi, there, feller." It was Tad, and Jimmy realized that Nancy was dressed for the street. He said hastily, "Sorry to hold you up — Well, 'by."

"Wait," called Nancy. "We're going to the

Greek's and a movie. Want to come along?"

"No, thanks," he called, and ran down the stairs.

On the street, he halted. Where to go, what to do? Back to the flat and have them say, "So, she stood you up!" Well, he supposed he had to eat. He'd go somewhere for dinner and see another picture. Something, anything, to kill time. He was bruised and sore because Nancy was sorry for him. And he was sick of being led around by the nose, he told himself savagely.

He went to a place where he could set his foot on a bar rail and drank three Manhattans in rapid succession. With the third he forgot that Nancy was sorry for him and that Tad was probably laughing at him now, across a table for two. He began to think about Lina instead, and of Bill Ryder. He left the bar and went to a table in the restaurant and recklessly ordered steak and French frieds. But when they came he didn't want them. He sat there and saw Lina, in Bill Ryder's arms, dancing somewhere, looking up at him and laughing. . . .

After a while he paid his check and went out. He wasn't drunk. He wished he were. He was simply so damned unhappy that the liquor hadn't done much but sharpen his awareness and his emotions and his imagination.

Lina — Lina. . . .

She wasn't, as it happened, having a very good time. Bill Ryder spent money freely, and his conversation was freer. It kept her on her toes to hold him within bounds. True he was good-looking enough, and he danced well and he always took her to places which were full of laughter and light, color and movement. But she was, she told herself grimly, taking this evening for her own ultimate good, as one would take a peculiarly unpleasant medicine, disguised with, say, orange juice.

"How's our little businesswoman?"

"I'm swell, Bill."

"And the boy friend?"

"Oh, he's all right too," she said carelessly, "if you mean Jimmy Hall."

"Still the one and only?"

"What do you think?" she asked, smiling slowly.

She was that way with Bill Ryder. Provocative, quick on the uptake, all her wits about her. That's how he liked his girls. And a girl was crazy not to give 'em all what they liked, up to a certain point. Nor did it suit her book to be too confidential. You could let Mr. Ryder assume that Jimmy was a heavy suitor, but beyond that you let him assume nothing. You didn't say, "I'm going to marry him." Not if you were in your right mind.

Ryder said, after a while, "I heard about your new job. Congratulations."

"Thanks," she said, and smiled at him again. She was looking extremely pretty. She wore a little more lipstick than she did when she went out with Jimmy, she had brushed her hair back from her forehead and ears and permitted it to curl about her neck. She was, and knew it, the prettiest girl in the room, although her frock had cost nineteen-fifty and her slippers had seen far better days.

"You ought to bring yourself to the attention of the advertising agency," said Ryder expansively.

"And how does one do that?" she inquired, laughing.

"Oh, there are ways," he replied. "I understand there's a conference with them pretty soon at Americo."

She laughed again and lifted her glass. There were bubbles in it, nice pale amber bubbles. She asked gayly, "I suppose I'm to hide under the table?"

Ryder shook his head at her. He said, "You're smart, Lina. *Verbum sap.*"

"With me as the sap?"

"No, darling. Look here. Welles is a hard nut to crack. Bates isn't. If you can get to him, it can be done."

"Thanks," she said carelessly, "for the tip. When I'm president of Americo I'll remember your words. Stepping stones to success."

They laughed, and presently he said, "Let's dance."

She was home by two o'clock. Her feet hurt and her slippers were ruined. But perhaps this time it was worth it. Nancy woke when she came in and murmured something about

29

Jimmy. So he'd been there, had he? "Mad as a hatter," mumbled Nancy. Well, so much the better, thought Lina, easing herself into bed. There'd been a little trouble with Ryder in the taxi. Not much, but just enough. And he'd said, angrily, "I don't know why I bother with you, Lina. You show me the door for three months; then you whistle me back. I know you well enough to believe there's a reason. You can't fool me. I'm not in love with you. But I'm sort of nuts about you. And you're about as friendly, after a certain point, as a bunch of cactus."

She laughed a little, in the darkness, thinking of that.

Just because she'd let him kiss her once or twice, before Jimmy. Not after, never after.

Well, she thought, setting her little jaw, she had gone out with Ryder. And she'd go out with him again, and again; until Jimmy came to his senses, until he saw things her way. If he wanted her, there was only one way to have her. He knew it. Why didn't he take that way? Why was he so stubborn, so miserably obstinate?

They could be so happy, if only he'd listen to reason. Now the happiness of being together was spoiled by this incessant conflict between them, and the occasional feeling that, after all, she might not be infallible. Then there was the terrifying realization, which came to her sometimes and stopped her breath, that life was unexpected and that things happened sometimes to people, even to young people, even to people like herself and Jimmy, healthy, vital people. You caught a cold, and it didn't seem anything to worry about, and then suddenly it was pneumonia. Or you crossed a street and a car tore around the corner. . . .

Sometimes she dreamed that Jimmy had died, and woke up sobbing with Nancy shaking her, and the sweat cold on her body and the tears warm on her cheeks. Sometimes she dreamed she was alone, lost, looking for Jimmy, calling for him, and he would or could not answer. That was bad too. And now and then they were together with other youngsters and she saw a girl, any girl, tilt her head up and smile at him in the intimate, seeking, surrendering way of some girls, she would feel faint and furious and terribly frightened. Suppose Jimmy met someone who wouldn't mind that thirty-five a week, who wouldn't think ahead to hardships and makeshifts and possible disaster, one who'd want Jimmy enough to —

Didn't she want him enough?

No, she told herself, lying there still and straight on the old couch. No, not enough to risk their happiness, to risk the gradual wearing away of their love. Not enough — and too much.

She turned on her side and closed her mind to Jimmy. The booklet on which she was currently engaged had to do with "Jelly Joy." This was relatively a newcomer to the Americo food

31

family. Originally conceived and manufactured by a small concern, Americo had bought it because of its proved excellence. But it was untried, compared with their other products, and it had, of course, plenty of competition. Lina wondered, beginning to feel drowsy, if she could interest them in her idea for a smaller package for a family of, say, two or three. She remembered something Jimmy had said, a couple of weeks ago — about the bride Kit had encountered in a retail store, complaining because she felt she wasted some of the gelatine in its present form. "After all," she'd said, "we don't want to eat it *every* night."

Jimmy again. She shut her eyes and, through sheer determination, slept.

The next day at the office Lina worked doggedly, deaf to the activity around her. The room was large, with row upon row of desks. Typewriters clattered, people rushed through, hands full of papers, compacts clicked at the lunch hour and the girls rose chattering and streamed into the restrooms and then out to lunch. Lina went down to the cafeteria and found Nancy already there, her lunch before her. Lina's tray bore a salad, milk, a portion of cottage cheese. She took it down the aisle and set it at the place Nancy was keeping for her and looked sternly at Nancy's selection, chocolate and whipped cream, peanut butter sandwiches, cake and more whipped cream.

"What about that ten pounds?"

"I know," said Nancy guiltily, "but honest, Lina, I'm starved. Yelland's on the warpath this morning and there's nothing like Yelland on the warpath to give me an appetite. I bet," she said, stirring the chocolate, "she had a row with the ball and chain last night. Married women are the devil to work for; they sure take it out on the hired help."

She lifted the cup and drank hastily, aware too late that she might be starting another argument. But Lina wasn't listening. She was thinking of her work. It hadn't gone any too well. She had spoken to her immediate superior about the small-package idea and he had not taken to it. He had a dozen arguments against it. But there must be a way in which you could work it out. Perhaps, she thought, a package containing small portions of each flavor, just enough in each one to make a dessert for two? After all, there were hundreds and thousands of women in the country who had to cook for two ninety-nine per cent of the time. Cooking for two, buying for two, without waste and without monotony, wasn't as easy as it sounded. She thought, *Of course I can't go over Welles's head obviously . . . but if I can get to Bates?*

Bates was the head of her department. She cut lunch short and deliberately returned to the office twenty minutes later. *Perhaps he hasn't gone yet,* she thought.

He had not. He had been busy and now he was on his way. There were only a few people in the room as he went past the rows of desks and he was paying attention to none. He was thinking of a number of things, of a poker game that had gone well the night before, and of Junior's first, remarkable tooth and of the fact that on Friday he and Mrs. Bates were going away for the week-end, and that at last they had found a responsible nurse for the only baby in the world, one with whom they would feel secure in leaving him. He was, therefore, in an amiable mood when Lina, rising from her desk, spoke to him.

He knew her, of course. She had been recommended to his attention by Welles and he had consented to give her the trial job on the promotion booklet. He had not regretted it, and she seemed extraordinarily serious about her work. He halted and smiled at her. She was worth a smile. Bates was a man whose married life was happy, but even such a paragon was bound to recognize, impersonally or otherwise, Lina's charm. And so he asked pleasantly, "Well, Miss Lawrence?"

"I know you're awfully busy," Lina told him; "it's just that . . . I've an idea . . . on Jelly Joy. It may not be worth anything but I thought, if you could give me five minutes?"

Bates looked at his watch. He was half an hour late now. He could afford another five minutes. He said, still smiling, "Well, if it's only five . . ."

Lina followed him back into his office. She

said, when he was seated at the desk, leaning back, waiting, with that air of indulgence a businessman has for a pretty woman, "I won't take three."

She had all the figures on Jelly Joy at her fingertips. She knew the selling points — she had talked them over with Jimmy a thousand times. She knew the obstacles the product encountered; that a big advertising campaign was being planned.

Bates listened, and made a few notes. He shook his head dubiously over her suggestion of the one-meal package. It might work, and again it might not. People often felt that they didn't get their money's worth. But it was something to consider, he admitted. When, the five minutes up, he went with her to the door and back to her desk, he said, "We're having a conference in ten days with the advertising agency. You've worked hard on Jelly Joy, Miss Lawrence. I'd like you to be present at the meeting. I'll let you know when."

Lina sat down at her desk. Her heart sang, her eyes were bright. The girl who had the desk next to hers strolled in, her beret in her hand, her fingertips pushing her finger wave into more seductive undulations. She commented, startled, "You look as if someone had left you a million."

"Better than that," said Lina. "Two."

She glanced at her notes and went to work. She thought, *Wait till I tell Jimmy!*

She did not tell him for almost a week. She grew edgy, waiting. Nancy suggested once, "Why don't you call him up?" and Lina snapped at her, "Don't be stupid; only a fool calls up first."

She went out with Ryder twice during that time. She said nothing to him of the conversation with Bates. It was not clever to permit a man to know he had helped you. Not that he had, really. She would have made an opportunity to talk to Bates without Bill Ryder's suggestion, sooner or later, she assured herself.

On Saturday, late in the afternoon, Jimmy called her. He asked, trying to be casual, "How about dinner tonight?" and she answered, as casually, "All right, Jimmy. Six-thirty, as usual?"

They went to Antonio's and their waiter, who had missed them, was solicitous. Lina, her eyes enormous and her color high, talked breathlessly. Ryder was for the moment ignored, and the time that had elapsed since their last meeting. She said, ending her story, "It's a chance . . . I mean, just the fact that Bates recognized I have something to offer. If only he doesn't forget he's asked me to come to the meeting!"

"Why should he?" asked Jimmy. "He'd be a helluva businessman if he did. He didn't suggest it in the first place because of your bright eyes or the color of your hair — or did he?" he inquired, frowning.

"Don't be silly," said Lina, "he doesn't know I exist, as a person."

36

"I'm not so sure," said Jimmy. "How could he help it? How could you help letting him know?"

"If you mean that I use — well — sex appeal, in business!" began Lina, irritated.

Jimmy said, "Look here, don't let's start anything. You do, of course. Hold on, I don't say you do *consciously*. I'm sure you don't. Forget it. Lina, I've been lower than banking figures lately. We can't go on like this."

She looked at him and her heart pounded sickeningly. No, he wasn't joking, it wasn't a gag. For a split second everything hung in the balance. Either he was — through — or she had won. It must be that she had won; she'd been so sure, she knew him so well. She had to win. She wanted him, she must have him — on her own terms.

She asked quietly, "What do you mean?"

"Ryder," he answered, flushed, and looked away. "I — I can't stand it, Lina. I've had a rotten time. My mind tries to convince me that it doesn't mean anything. But I'm afraid. Afraid you'll get too used — oh, not to Ryder, he doesn't matter, he's just a symbol — but to doing without me, being without me. We can't go on quarreling. I can't believe you're right, yet I've no business to dream that you'd make a sacrifice for me; perhaps women don't make such sacrifices any more, perhaps they weren't sacrifices in other days but —"

She interrupted sharply, "What *are* you talking about?"

He smiled at her, crookedly. "I'm trying to tell you it's okay with me. It's got to be. If you won't take me on what I'm making then — keep your job, Lina, but marry me, soon," he said.

It was over, and she had won. She could afford to be kind, sweet, to lull his every doubt, to transport him. That evening they broke their convention of not going to her place when Nancy was out, and went there for a while, to make their plans. Lina made these, in a warm rush of enthusiasm, laughter, caresses. Once, coming a little to himself, he said, "But there's one string to it, Lina. When I'm making enough — when I'm district manager, you'll quit? That will be five thousand — when I make that . . . ?"

She would have promised anything. A district managership seemed a long way off. She put her arms about him, kissed him ardently. "Darling, of course!" she pledged.

He wasn't sure. He didn't believe her. His uncertainty was so strong that she could feel it; it reached out from him, exasperated, terrified her. She looked at him and in that instant he thought, with so keen a certainty that it was a knife-edge of understanding, *I'm crazy, she doesn't mean it, she means to have her way, she'll promise anything to shut me up. It isn't too late, not even though I've committed myself —*

He thought this and hardly knew that he did so, for she was in his arms again, all her weight against him, and there was fever in her hands touching his face, drawing his mouth to her mouth. And she was saying brokenly the things she had not said to him before, saying that she wanted him, that she couldn't live without him, that she was his own — his *own*. . . .

The lamplight blurred before his eyes, and he was in a singing darkness. He could not think; he was aware of nothing but this surrendering creature, this girl who embodied for him all the terror and beauty and wonder of flame. And when, presently, he held her away from him and said, with a half laugh which had nothing of merriment in it, "Look here, woman — I've got to be on my way, or else —" and saw her eyes, clouded with love and with something very like gratitude, he experienced pride, in himself and in his restraint and in his love which compelled restraint, and did not know that it was her will that he put her aside and say just that, nor that she knew both when and how to do so, and when, too, to be grateful.

He thought of nothing but her yielding and his care of her. And his mind at least was satisfied. His doubts seemed foolish. She loved him. He had her word; she would keep it. He would work like hell.

"Let's get married next week," he told her, but she laughed at him. There were a hundred things to consider. Nancy would have to find a roommate. They must look for an apartment, shop . . .

In a month then. Presently he went home, a man who would be married in a month's time, who tried to persuade himself that in reality he had surrendered nothing of his pride, his male integrity. Lina was the important thing. Nothing else mattered, basically.

Lina, waiting for Nancy to come in, was thinking herself the happiest woman in the world, the most triumphant. She experienced an amazing, almost terrifying sense of power. When Nancy came in she'd tell her. She'd say, "See! See, Nancy, how right I was — ? It worked like a charm, just as I knew it would!"

Chapter Three:

TO US — WITH DIFFERENCES

"And where," asked Nancy, a day later, "are you going on your honeymoon?"

She was torn between her personal loss and romantic excitement. Of course, it had been only a question of time before one of them would go. But Nancy had believed she would be that one — considering Lina's conflict with Jimmy. Nancy had placed her money on Jimmy. It was a shock to discover that he, like most men, could be persuaded into a decision against his principles. It gave her a mixed feeling of vicarious triumph in the capabilities of her own, and tolerant contempt for Jimmy's, sex.

"It's all planned," replied Lina briskly. "We'll be married on a Friday evening and go home. There won't be any honeymoon until summer, when we'll hope to wangle the same vacations. You and Tad will go with us, won't you — to the minister's? Kit and Alice will come too."

"Well," said Nancy helplessly, "a wedding without a honeymoon!" She sighed and then inquired hopefully, "What about Atlantic City?"

Lina shook her head, smiling. "Can't afford it," she said cheerfully; "you forget we're working people." She looked up from the desk-bureau at which she was writing notes to a chosen few, and laughed at Nancy's disconsolate face. "Cheer up," she advised, "you just can't get away from the old idea of showers and parties, church weddings and Niagara Falls, can you?"

"No," admitted Nancy defiantly, "and I don't want to. When I marry Tad I'm going back to South Bend and have me a wedding with all the trimmings. After all, you can have only one."

"I've heard otherwise," suggested Lina.

Nancy snorted. "Only one with orange blossoms and a veil," she answered definitely.

Lina sealed the last of her envelopes. She commented, "You've been reading Emily Post again."

Nancy wasn't listening. She asked, "What about your ring?"

Lina looked down at her slim hands. She said slowly, "I'll have one, of course. Plain gold. I suppose that's up your alley — it's sentimental enough. But I won't be able to wear it to work."

"Aren't you going to tell them at the office?" Nancy asked, astonished.

"No. Jimmy and I talked it over. He's against my not telling, naturally, but" — she shrugged slightly — "what's the use? With so many unmarried girls out of jobs —"

"I get you," said Nancy. She added gloomily, "I wish Yelland would get the ax. Talk about Thanksgiving!"

"She's been with Americo for years," Lina reminded her; "that's different."

"Well, you know best," agreed Nancy dubiously. "What about an engagement ring?"

"Not yet," said Lina. "We had to choose between furniture and a ring. You can't set a ring for dinner, or sit in it evenings or toss up an omelette on it. The savings must go for furniture and darned little of that." She reflected, frowning. Then she said, "I'm afraid I'll have to take my things."

Nancy nodded. "Okay," she said briefly, "I'll manage."

"But you can't alone!"

"There's Mabel Thane," said Nancy, "from home. She's working at Mapes and Masters, and living at a club. I ran into her last week and she said she was looking for someone to share a place. I'll get in touch with her. I hated her like poison in the fifth grade because her hair curled and mine didn't, but I guess I can overlook that now — with the help of curlers and a little lotion."

"Good," said Lina, relieved. Not that she and Nancy were close; they weren't. Their association was based on economic necessity and it was sheer luck that they happened to like each other and to get along well.

The rest of the time was one of feverish activity. Lina was present at the conference with the advertising agency, spoke her little piece for Jelly Joy and acquitted herself with credit. Bates congratulated her afterward. He said, "You've

43

done a good job. The agency representative recognized it and was really impressed."

Evenings, she rushed home to supper, sometimes with Jimmy and sometimes with Nancy, and once or twice Nancy and Tad came along with them to Antonio's. Tad was an alert young man with a double cowlick, a slight but engaging impediment in his speech, and so much vitality that Lina always felt drained and empty after she had been with him for long. Luckily Nancy was not affected in the same way; she was far too placid for that.

The flat hunting was not as easy. The Americo office was in midtown and Lina had hoped to find a place near by, but it was beyond her budget. Jimmy disagreed. He assumed seventy dollars a week between the two of them was ample and assured her that all the best experts claimed that one week's salary is equal to one month's rent.

"Not nowadays," contradicted Lina, "I don't want to pay more than forty."

After a long search she found a midtown apartment on the East Side, not far enough uptown to be fashionable, for fifty dollars a month.

The lease signed, arrangements made, she and Jimmy went shopping on evenings when the stores were open late. They bought the minimum that, with her furniture, would do. Nancy gave them an end table, Kit contributed a radio. Lina's upstate relatives sent a check, as did Jimmy's Philadelphia cousins.

Trying to move and work and be married all, it seemed, at the same time proved difficult. Lina grew thin and nervous, and in the midst of absorbing the advertising agency's research on Jelly Joy she would find herself wondering if perhaps red-checked gingham in the kitchen hadn't been a mistake.

Jimmy had a battered armchair and a smoking stand which he could call his own, and a tumbled heap of books. He also had a bright idea. Kit's girl was one of those unusual young women who not only had no job, but who desired none. She lived in a comfortable house in Flatbush with her parents, and enjoyed housekeeping.

Lina liked her and when Jimmy suggested that Alice might oversee the moving for them, Lina seized upon the straw. "Do you suppose she would — ? Oh, but it's too much to ask!"

"She'll love it," prophesied Jimmy, "and so will Kit. It may put her in the proper frame of mind to listen to him."

Privately Lina doubted that. Not, she thought, if Alice had good sense. Kit was so impractical, and without ambition. He came of a very well-to-do family in Cleveland with whom he had quarreled because of an unfortunate marriage contracted in his junior year in college and ending in divorce six months later, and, refusing to return to the rather austere family bosom, had finally become a detail salesman for Americo.

Alice proved delighted and Lina went on with her job, knowing that Alice was at the apartment making herself extremely useful.

Three evenings before their marriage Lina and Jimmy met at the apartment. The gateleg table shone, from its corner. Linen and silver were in the desk-bureau, pots and pans hung in the proper cupboards. Lina's old gilt mirror was placed at exactly the right angle in the living-room. The bedroom was settled to the last tie-back curtain. Jimmy's books were in the bookcase and Alice's gift — two good small etchings — was on the wall. And the kitchen pantry was stocked.

Lina sat down on the divan in the living-room. In the flat she was sleeping on a cot which Mabel had sent over. She said, smiling, "Well — thanks to Alice —"

"She's a peach," said Jimmy. He threw his cigarette away and came to sit beside her, his arm about her shoulders. "Lina, is it real? Will we be at home — Friday evening?"

"We will."

His clasp tightened. He said slowly, "I hope to God you'll never be sorry, Lina."

"Sorry?" She looked at him, laughing, for a moment. Then her face grew grave. She put her slender hands on either side of his face and kissed him. She said, "How could anyone as happy as I'm going to be ever be sorry?"

"That's all that matters," he told her.

Presently she said, "I thought Alice and Kit

were coming up and we were going out and have something to eat?"

"Gosh!" said Jimmy. "I forgot." He looked stricken. "Kit's been called home. They got him on the phone early this morning. His father's very ill."

"Oh, I'm so sorry," said Lina. "How long since he has seen him?"

"Three — four years. I'm not sure. He flew, much as he hates planes."

"Perhaps he'll go into his father's office," said Lina. "It would mean more money. And, probably, Alice."

"I don't think Alice thinks much about money," said Jimmy. "And I was thinking of his people. Must have been pretty hard on his mother."

"I suppose so," said Lina absently. Jimmy, looking at her, marveled at her lack of perception. She did seem so terribly self-sufficient. It wasn't really her fault. He wondered for the thousandth time whether she would continue to seem so after their marriage. He thought, *Something's haywire; it's as if she were a man, not thinking about permanent relationships.* He supposed himself different because of his background, his happy childhood, his memory of family life, his realization, even as a boy, of how close and fine the pattern, and how gay with love. His father and mother had been so much in love; but not selfishly; they had had plenty to spare for him. He told himself, grinning at the

47

absurdity, *Looks as if I were the domestic one in this ménage.*

"What are you smiling about?"

"Me? Oh, nothing," he said, rousing himself. "Let's go look in the kitchen again. By the way, can you cook?"

"Well," said Lina, "not — not marvelously. Don't look so downcast. I can boil an egg and fry some bacon and make some coffee — and there's always Jelly Joy," she added, and going into the kitchen with him, indicated the package on the shelf. "Now that I have to begin to think about variety in meals and waste in the garbage can, I could wish even harder that they'd fall for my inspiration of the one-meal package in each flavor."

"Did you tell 'em about it at the conference?" Jimmy wanted to know, wholly forgetting that it was he who had been responsible for the "inspiration."

"Of course; they looked wise and pulled their beards —"

"Beards! For Pete's sake!"

"Figuratively, darling. Anyway they um-ed and ah-ed and said 'very interesting, I'm sure,' and that was that. They seemed attracted by my figures. I don't know why. They've got an investigation and research department which is on its toes every minute."

"Forget Jelly Joy," ordered Jimmy. He pulled her back against him and ruffled her hair with his big hand. "Happy?"

"How about you?"

"You know," he said, and stood there a moment, at the kitchen window with its gay red-checked curtains, and looked down on the streets and the lights. He thought, *Every night, I'll be coming home — to Lina.*

But, he reminded himself presently when they had left the apartment and were walking toward Lexington Avenue in search of a buckwheat-and-coffee, *Maybe I won't be. Maybe I'll get home first and wait for her and suffer all the tortures of the damned wondering if she's been run over or taken ill on the street, or something. . . .*

That was Tuesday. Wednesday they did not see each other at all. Lina was busy packing her last things, as Thursday evening she planned the luxury of a shampoo, a wave, and a facial at one of the big shops. She had drawn heavily on her savings for a few new clothes, consoling herself with the thought that she would have enough to carry her through the summer.

Wednesday morning Jimmy telephoned.

"Lina? I've had a wire from Kit. His father died shortly after he reached home."

"Jimmy — I'm so sorry!"

"So am I. Alice is going out. When she comes home again Kit will come on and they'll be married. He's resigning his job and going into the family business."

She asked breathlessly, "Jimmy, is there any chance for you?"

He knew what she meant. "I don't know. I

hope so. I'll see Lloyd as soon as I can," he answered.

Lloyd was the head of the sales department. Presently Lina hung up, flushed and excited. *Poor Kit* . . . Oh, yes, of course, poor Kit, but the world is so constructed and human nature is so patterned that one man's misfortune may be another's opportunity. And it wasn't as if Kit hadn't double the opportunity for success now — a secure berth, a certain income.

She flew upstairs and burst into the room where Nancy sat talking with Mabel. Mabel was emulating the G-men and, by degrees, moving in.

"What's wrong?" asked Nancy.

"Nothing; Kit's father's dead," said Lina, unconscious of the curious effect of that reply, "and he's not coming back. It may mean that Jimmy gets his job."

"That's more money," said Nancy practically; "if he does, will you resign yours?"

"Well, no!" cried Lina, astonished.

"But he'll be making more than —"

"I know," said Lina, "but that's just so much to the good. We can save. I — Oh, won't it be marvelous!"

She flew at Nancy and hugged her, to the latter's amazement, as Lina was not demonstrative. Nancy hugged back. She said, "Well, all the luck in the world, old girl, but I never thought you'd marry a missionary!"

On Thursday morning Lina looked up to see

the manager of her section by her desk. He told her, "Mr. Bates wants to see you, Miss Lawrence," and Lina remarked his speculative regard. Yet his face was otherwise unreadable.

On the way to the office she thought, *Perhaps he's heard — about Jimmy?* If so, it might mean that she would be let out. It wouldn't be fair, she reminded herself; she had worked hard, she was ambitious. What difference could it make to Americo? The argument against married women in offices came to her, and she ignored them. Hadn't she a right to earn a living? What if there were hundreds of unemployed young women, with themselves to support or their parents as well? She'd made her own place, hadn't she? Fought for it and filled it. It wasn't just that she should have to relinquish it just because she was young and human and in love. The nervous tears invaded her eyes and she brushed them away before she knocked on Mr. Bates's door.

His secretary opened to her, murmured, "Mr. Bates is expecting you," and slipped past to her desk in the outer room in which Lina stood. Lina went in. Mr. Bates looked up from his desk and smiled at her. "Sit down, Miss Lawrence, I have something to discuss with you."

Twenty minutes later when she returned to her desk her color was brilliant. Her hands shook as she inserted paper and carbon in her machine. The giddy young thing at the next desk muttered sympathetically, "What happened . . . bad medicine?"

Lina shook her head, smiling. Her lips were unsteady. She couldn't believe her luck. Yet it wasn't luck; even Mr. Bates had said it was a reward of merit. "Of course," he'd added, "we'll be sorry to lose you, but we've no right to stand in your way, and after all, you'll still be working for us, in the last analysis."

She wouldn't tell anyone yet except Jimmy. But she must tell him — as soon as possible. She hadn't planned to see him tonight; she'd arranged to go straight to the beauty salon from work, after a malted milk and a sandwich around the corner.

During the facial the operator asked, "Can't you relax? You're so terribly tense."

She couldn't, nor could she enjoy the luxurious sensation of skilled fingers patting her face, molding her chin line, or the flower scents of cream and lotion.

She had telephoned Jimmy's apartment from a drugstore and left a message. She thought, *Perhaps he didn't get it, perhaps he won't come.* It seemed to her that if he didn't come she couldn't endure it.

But he was there, waiting outside the shop, the big shop with the charmingly dressed windows and the placard in one of them: *Open Wednesdays, Thursdays, and Fridays till 9 p.m. for the convenience of businesswomen.*

"Jimmy — !"

"Lina — I had your message. I was going to the flat anyway and take my chances on being thrown out — I had to see you. Look, I've talked to Lloyd over the phone — he says —"

"Jimmy, wait!" She stood there with her hand on his arm and her eager face upturned to his, radiant, almost crying with excitement, "I've something to tell you —"

"Yes, but Lloyd said —"

"Oh, *please* listen! The advertising agency wants me. They've asked Mr. Bates for me. I'm to go to them the first of the month — to work on the Jelly Joy account — at fifty a week. To *start!* And the sky's the limit!" An expert copy writer could earn far more than fifty a week. In a year, two years, she might be earning four thousand annually, in five years, she might earn five, six, ten . . .

"Jimmy," she demanded, "aren't you *glad?*"

Her voice was sharp with urgency, disappointment. He stood there staring at her in the light from the street lamps. He said, "Of course . . . but . . . that makes my news a little flat."

She was instantly all contrition. "I'm sorry," she told him; "what is it, darling?"

"Just that I'm to have Kit's place. . . . It — it's a step up."

He'd been so proud, so — so damned relieved. The extra money would mean he'd top her salary and might mean that after a while he could persuade her to quit — for surely she'd believe him on the road to something approximating real success now? But her luck had held with his. They were even again, or was she in the lead? And in a blinding flash he saw that her way lay open and clear before her while his ran to a dead-end street. After district salesman, there wasn't much hope. You didn't get to be an executive, not likely. Oh, it happened to a few, the unusual ones. He wasn't one of them. He'd work like a nailer in Kit's job and perhaps, after a long time, a district salesmanship would be open. But after — ? He laughed aloud. He couldn't say, *"Watch my smoke, I'll be president some day."* Things didn't happen like that in real life.

She was telling him how glad she was, that it was wonderful, it was a good omen for both of them. And then suddenly she was crying noiselessly, the tears running down her cheeks.

"Lina, darling!" he said, aghast.

"I'm all right — just too much excitement. Let's go down to Antonio's, Jimmy, and have something to eat. I had only a sandwich early, and I'm starved."

So now here they were, the night before their wedding, sitting at their regular table at Antonio's, later than was their custom.

Jimmy said, "Look here, Lina, I didn't mean — It's swell, and you deserve it. Only I thought I was Santa Claus, see? And you knocked the pins right out from under me. This — this will make a difference. You're going to town, you're on your way —"

He thought, *I've swallowed having a wife who*

earns as much as I do, but when it comes to one who earns more . . . ?

"But it mustn't make a difference," she told him; "It can't. Why should it? We'll work together, and save and — oh, Jimmy," she smiled at him, her eyes clear and luminous, "we'll have such a *grand* time. It's so much better this way. Things to talk about, beyond housekeeping and headlines. Allied work. And it's my big chance. Surely you don't begrudge it to me?"

"No," he said soberly, but with his crooked smile, "no, of course not. I'm — I'm pretty damned proud of you! Lina — ?"

Clatter and noise all about them, people passing between the crowded tables, a girl's overhigh laughter, a man calling out to a friend, smoke eddying. . . .

"Yes, Jimmy?"

"You know — I just want you to be happy."

"I know. And I am," she said earnestly.

Their waiter brought them the usual red wine. Jimmy closed his hand about his glass. He informed the waiter, "We're going to be married tomorrow."

The waiter exclaimed. He snatched the glasses away. "One second," he said, beaming, " 'scusa — one second —"

He departed, with the glasses. Jimmy and Lina looked at each other, laughed, puzzled. "What in the world," began Lina.

"Never mind. Do you love me?"

"Of course."

55

The fat waiter returned, hurrying with more glasses. There was wine in them, sound sweet sherry. "Ona the house," he explained, triumphant. "I tella the boss and he say, 'Tella these young people —' "

But they were not listening. He shrugged himself away, washed his hands of them, thought, rushing to another table, *For a little while they come perhaps and then no more, not after they have the bambino and go out no more to Antonio's for dinner.*

Lina raised her glass.

"It's not going to make a difference? Nothing will make a difference, ever?"

"Not ever," he promised.

They touched glasses, and laughed. They were suddenly carefree, very highhearted.

"To us," said Jimmy.

"To us," said Lina.

The glasses clashed again, their eyes met, their smiling, ardent regard was merged. But Jimmy was thinking, *Is it right, shall I be able to hold her, shall I ever convince myself this is the way?* And Lina was exulting, in a wild upsurge of triumph, *I knew it! It's been so easy, after all — and exactly as I planned.*

If only she's happy, thought Jimmy. *To You!* said his eyes, his misgivings momentarily stifled. *To Me!* thought Lina, in her secret heart. Yet, raising their glasses, they said, simultaneously:

"To us!"

Chapter Four:

NO TIME FOR LOVE

On the first of June Lina entered the advertising agency of Harcourt, Lowell, and Shaw and was assigned to work on the Jelly Joy copy of the important Americo account.

She had no misgivings. She had believed for a long time that she could write better than average copy and she felt, with considerable truth, that she was closer to this particular product than anyone in the outside agency. During the week-end before her new job began, Jimmy complained bitterly that he had married a package of gelatine in unexcelled fruit flavors.

Lina laughed at him and paid no heed. If at the movies Saturday night, during a sultry love scene, her attention was not upon Fröken Garbo, if she was but vaguely aware of Jimmy's handclasp, she was not, she asserted over a drugstore counter soda afterward, to blame. After all, it was important, wasn't it, that she have all the Jelly Joy facts at her fingertips?

"Sure," conceded Jimmy, and grinned at her. She was so small and eager and so devastatingly pretty, and she could be, as he well knew, incomparably sweet. "Sure it's important. But honest, Lina, it's something of a blow just when I'm getting romantic and about to whisper that Greta hasn't a thing on you, to hear you sud-

57

denly hiss, 'Jimmy, do you remember the exact sales figures for last week in your district?' "

Lina applied her red mouth to her straw and drew up the last lingering sweetness of chocolate and vanilla. She said, after a minute, "But you can always tell me that! We've lots of time for pretty speeches, all our lives."

She was sure of this, and of him. She was sure of her hold over his heart, his mind, and his senses. And it irritated her to discover him less serious about her new position than she was. He regarded it with a distaste he was unable to conceal, but which she felt confident would soon yield to familiarity. She forgot that familiarity breeds contempt.

They were, on the whole, very happy. Lina was a neat and efficient housekeeper. She had had a hard training in the big, old-fashioned houses of her upstate relatives, and once she had established a schedule the care of a small apartment was child's play.

She didn't, however, carry the entire burden; nor did she see any reason why she should. She was as much a wage earner as Jimmy; they were in the deepest sense partners. There was no reason why she should do everything. So young Mr. Hall rose first and started breakfast, and sometimes if young Mrs. Hall was very tired, or headachy or out of sorts, he fixed a tray with her coffee and toast and orange juice and brought it to her and consumed his own meal, fortified by a couple of eggs, sunny side up, in the kitchen nook where they always ate unless they had company. And sometimes if he arrived home earlier than she, he started dinner. His knowledge of cooking had been confined to camping trips which he had enjoyed in earlier days, but it improved. More than once Lina came home from work to find him with an apron tied around his middle, a look of determination on his face, his red hair standing up in all directions and a cookbook clutched in his hands. This was the direct result of an argument they had had on sex superiority, during the first week of their married life.

It began over an editorial which exhorted women to flee offices and concentrate upon the home. Lina snorted gently. "Written by a man, of course," she commented, tossing the paper aside. "He's as antediluvian as those what-you-may-call-'em eggs they discovered in the Gobi Desert."

"Maybe he has the dope, at that," suggested Jimmy, wrestling with his pipe. Well fed, comfortable, he looked about the pleasant living-room with approval.

"I believe you smoke matches, not tobacco," she said. "What do you mean, he may be right?"

"The world wagged along nicely," Jimmy reminded her, "and for a long time, on the theory that woman's place was in the home."

She said quickly, "Jimmy, you aren't going to begin that again?"

He shook his head, *That is one of the troubles with women*, he thought; *you can't discuss any-*

thing with them — they have to take it personally or not at all. "I'm just discussing the facts of life in the abstract," he assured her.

Lina said, after a moment, "Look at the professions open to women now — which were once considered sacred to men. Medicine, law, even engineering and theology. As for business, there's no holding them."

"Agreed," said Jimmy placidly; "but for one woman who is a professional or business success, you have a thousand men. The percentage is still to the male, Lina, don't forget that. And there are few professions in which women excel men, remember. I can think of just one at the moment. Nursing."

"How about teaching?"

"Fifty-fifty," said Jimmy firmly, "or forty-sixty. Sixty to my sex."

"Cooking?" cried Lina.

"Chefs," said Jimmy with dignity, "are men. The finest cooks in the world."

Lina giggled. "I'd like to see you confronted with a dinner to get, Jimmy Hall."

"Confront me," he said grandly. "I'll rise to the occasion. Go on."

"Dress designing?" suggested Lina.

"Men again," said Jimmy, "dozens of 'em. The best in the nation, or any nation. All the big names, almost. Men! There's one thing you can beat us at, of course," he said, "just one thing you can do and we can't."

"What's that?" asked Lina, already tiring of

the discussion, her mind wandering to the problem of a new cleaning woman. Their present weekly slave was most unsatisfactory.

"Motherhood," replied Jimmy solemnly.

"Oh, that," said Lina carelessly, and laughed as if he had said something very funny indeed. Jimmy watched her move about the room, straightening things up, looking along the bookshelves for the volume on advertising to which she had recently treated herself. He thought, *A kid might make a difference — it does to most women — But Lina doesn't want a baby — that is, she says she doesn't. She's wrong, most likely. She just won't admit it, because of her job. If she didn't have a job . . . ?*

But she had one and liked it. She went into the agency determined to conquer any obstacles which she might encounter. She was aware that there might be resentment among those already established there. There is usually a feeling against someone brought in from outside, stepped up from one job to a better job, over the heads perhaps of people who have been working in an office for some years. They might resent, too, her introduction as a species of expert, even if it was only Jelly Joy on which she was supposed to be the last word.

There were ways to dissipate resentment. Lina watched her step, with both her clear gray eyes. She liked the great offices high over Park Avenue; she liked the activity, the sense of excitement, alertness — the space salesmen waiting in the reception room, the telephones ringing, the discussion of campaigns, consumer reaction, feminine angles, all the jargon of the business, the talk of surveys and dealer approach and percentages. She liked the people with whom she came in contact. Howard, the copy chief, thin, haggard, dynamic, who, it was whispered, drank more than was good for him but not during working hours; George Onslow, erratic, the highest paid of the copy writers, next in line to Howard, good-looking, a little too well dressed, with, Lina discovered shortly, a roving eye. And she liked Beatrice Harris, the only other woman assigned to the Americo account.

Miss Harris was twenty-seven years old. She earned in the neighborhood of eight thousand a year, and worked on much of the copy that went out for Americo. When Lina came into the agency she was concentrating on Champion Flour, and while swearing, in a virile and accomplished manner, under her breath, was turning out the most perfect of copy, calculated to sell the thrifty housewife at first sight.

Lina had her own office, a tiny cubbyhole, with a desk, a chair, a typewriter, a wastebasket, and a window. Miss Harris's office adjoined hers and was on a much more magnificent scale. Beatrice rated a secretary while Lina, if necessary, must call on the services of one or the other of half a dozen typists with roving commissions.

It wouldn't be hard, thought Lina, to disarm Howard, with his savage scowl and nervous, shy grin; it would be the work of a moment, so to speak, to enlist George Onslow on her side. She hadn't been with the agency more than three days before she learned that a fleeting display of leg, a slow, reluctant smile, and uplifted, admiring eyes would serve to fasten Mr. Onslow's amiable attention. But, as for Beatrice Harris — ?

For the first couple of weeks their contact was limited to a mere greeting. Then one day Lina, with her copy in one hand, knocked on Beatrice's door.

When she went in she found Miss Harris smoking furiously and throwing things on the floor. From the general welter of untidiness and out of the haze of smoke she emerged, small, overthin, dark, with an unusual combination of features which would have been extraordinarily plain if she hadn't taken pains and shown genius in figuratively rearranging them. You did not notice the too-high cheekbones and the nose flaring at the nostrils, or the sallow skin. Instead, you saw enormous eyes, to which art called your attention, the scarlet slash of the big mouth, and the beautiful even teeth; you saw the clever hands and the thick cap of black hair, falling in a confusion of curly bangs to the blacker eyes. And you saw, if you were a woman, the custom-made frock, severe, daring, perfect. . . .

"Well?" barked Miss Harris.

Lina smiled at her, timidly. She said, disarmingly:

"I've come to be a nuisance. I suppose I have my nerve — but — look here, I'm *stuck*. I don't dare to admit it to Mr. Howard. . . . He liked the suggestions I made the first week I was here, told me to go ahead on my own. But now I'm — scared. I can't afford to fall down on this job, Miss Harris, and I do want a woman's opinion — so I thought — but, of course, you're terribly busy and I've no right . . . only — well," said Lina, with her engaging smile and with her gray eyes fixed, in something approximating worship, on Miss Harris — "you're so damned clever!"

Miss Harris pushed aside some more papers, waved a hand toward a chair and said, "Sit down. I'm in a tight spot myself. Here, let's have a look."

Five minutes later fair head and dark were close together. Miss Harris ticked off a sentence in Lina's copy with a red pencil. "No vitality," she said. "No punch. I wouldn't buy five cents' worth on the strength of that. This is better." She ticked off another phrase. "A lot better. I like it. Shorten this up, tighten it. Emphasize the appearance, the money saving. That's the combination that gets women. Looks better, costs less. I believe they're more concerned with that than with how a thing tastes. Sheep, all of 'em."

64

Lina listened and made notes. She had had no intention of using the appeal which Beatrice had crossed off her copy with the brutal red pencil. This copy had been arranged, not for Howard, the copy chief, but for Miss Harris. It contained plenty of mistakes. Miss Harris couldn't be expected to rejoice over a perfect piece of copy writing — when their acquaintance was so young.

Lina murmured her thanks and presently left. She said, at the door, "You — you're not a bit like I thought — I mean . . ." She caught herself up in a pretty embarrassment.

"Well, out with it," commanded Beatrice, amused; "what did you think?"

"I was simply terrified of you," confessed Lina frankly. Beatrice's laughter followed her from the room.

Nice little thing, thought Beatrice, going back to her job; *brains, too. And pretty,* she added justly. She wasn't afraid of women's looks. Appearances afforded her no competition. She had no illusions about her own. She couldn't be pretty, she hadn't the slightest claim to beauty. But she had something else. She knew it, and she made the most of it. She had charm and vitality for a dozen women. She washed them out, just being near them. And especially she wasn't afraid of blondes.

Lina shut the door to her own office, smiling. She tore up the copy she had shown Beatrice Harris and produced that which she would show Mr. Howard. She sat down at her desk and went to work. She was well satisfied. Beatrice might be clever — but she wasn't clever enough.

Beatrice Harris had a reputation, among advertising agencies and among her social circle. Her reputation as a good copy writer was merited. Her reputation as the Dorothy Parker of the agencies was not, to a great extent. She was, however, a past mistress of the wisecrack. She could discern unerringly the chink in the other fellow's armor and would, as likely as not, put her foot through it. She had been married and divorced. She had a great many men friends and a raft of women acquaintances. She disliked women; they irritated her, they were sentimental — or else even more unscrupulous than she. They were fools where men were concerned; they had no solidarity of purpose. They had, for the most part, unless a man was the reward, no fighting instinct, no intestinal fortitude. She had never made a woman friend without a motive. Now and then she met one whom she could employ as a social lever or as a foil. Otherwise, she called them all "darling" and despised them.

Some of the stories told about her were pure legend. No one could vouch for the fact that once she had climbed to a loft on which she had seen advertised from the street, *Everything sharpened which needs an edge* to inquire gently, "Are you sharpening wits today?" But everyone believed it.

At the end of July Beatrice Harris and Lina were lunching together once or twice a week and Beatrice had been to the apartment and met Jimmy.

She said, when she learned that Lina was married, "Why?"

"I was in love, Bea."

Beatrice groaned. "Lina, I thought you were — more accomplished. Of course, I suppose one has to get it out of one's system. I was just about your age when I did." She made a terrific and appalling face, as ugly as a devil mask, and then laughed. She had an entrancing laugh, deep, unexpected. "Well, more power to you, my dear. I'd like to meet him."

She liked him, when she did. She looked in upon Lina the following morning and inquired, "And how's our little jelly expert this sweltering summer day? I adore your young man. He's very attractive. I warn you, I'll try to get him away from you — temporarily. Or perhaps," she added thoughtfully, "I'd better wait six months or so. He's still as transparently a bridegroom as if he were wrapped in cellophane. By the way, I suppose you have realized that he can be very useful to you, in your job. He has a seat in the orchestra, you know."

Lina said quickly, "We don't talk business much, Bea. It's the least I can do — not burden him with it, his few free hours."

Beatrice grinned. She said, leaving, "Oh, yeah? You can't fool me, Lina. Howard showed

67

me that last piece of copy. Someone did a little missionary work on that or I'm a blonde with a clinging disposition."

Lina laughed, and the door closed. She didn't mind Beatrice knowing that Jimmy helped her — a little. Why shouldn't he? It was a partnership, wasn't it? But she would just as soon that Beatrice did not decide to enlist his services in the battle for Americo's other brands.

As detail salesman Jimmy visited the retail stores in his district, aided and abetted window dressing, saw that Americo brands were properly displayed, listened to complaints, of both grocer and consumer, checked up on stock, took orders, and often hunted out the research done by the house-to-house men, those members of the inquisition, gentlemen or ladies, armed with the questionnaires, and applied what they had learned to his own experience. Now and then he reproached Lina, halfheartedly.

"Look here, isn't it enough to have to report to Peterson and to be saddled with paper work and heaven knows what, without coming home and finding you all primed with leading questions?"

"Dearest," she said, and ruffled his hair and tweaked his ears and made him generally uncomfortable and happy, "I know I'm a pest. But I can't get along without you, can I?"

So she kissed him, half a dozen times or

more, and then sat down with paper and pencil to learn what Jelly Joy was doing in Williamsburg.

In August Jimmy was given his vacation. He had been confident that Lina would ask for two weeks at the same time. But she did not. She said, when he expostulated, "I don't *dare,* Jimmy. I'm getting along all right, but I've only been there since June. I can't ask for a vacation. I'll wait till I've been there six months or more —"

"What good will that do me? I can't change now, even if I wanted to — I have to take it when I can get it, Lina. I'd looked forward —" His voice was unsteady. He had planned it all: the camping trip in Maine; the fun they'd have, fishing, hiking; two solid weeks of being together, every moment of the twenty-four hours. No business. And Lina more completely his own than she had ever been, not coming home tired evenings, a little sharp, bored with the idea of going to the movies, fatigued at the thought of cooking. "I'm dead, Jimmy. The chops will keep till tomorrow. Let's go out somewhere. No, not Antonio's. It's too far downtown. Somewhere near."

"I'd counted on it —"

"So had I," she told him, and her eyes were suddenly misty. "Oh, don't be cross, Jimmy. Please! I'm just as disappointed as you are, but —"

"You've known all along that you wouldn't

ask to get away —"

"Perhaps. I was afraid to tell you; I knew how you'd planned. I — I kept hoping that I'd have the nerve. But I haven't. I do so want to make good, Jimmy."

So in the end he spent his vacation in town. Two interminably hot weeks, with the asphalt soft under foot and the sun brazen in the cloudless sky. He got up late and killed time as best he could. Now and then he persuaded Lina to meet him for lunch. Once she brought Beatrice Harris along, and once George Onslow stopped at their table and said, "So this is the dog in the manger, is it?" which Jimmy hadn't liked much. Onslow knew that Lina was married. Almost everyone in the agency knew it now, although it had not been announced officially. The agency didn't mind. But when the intelligence drifted back to Messrs. Welles and Bates of the Americo outfit, they were properly amazed. They hadn't dreamed it, they said.

It was Beatrice who advised against concealment.

"They'll know sooner or later. And they won't care. But if I were you, unless you want to get in a jam, I'd tell Georgie myself. It seems to me that he had strictly dishonorable hopes in your direction."

So Lina told George Onslow. She'd gone out to lunch with him and confided in him, timidly. "I'm not sure whether or not it will make a difference in the office," she said. "I hope not."

Was it her fault that George assumed her married status to be of longer standing than it really was, something in the nature of a girlish folly, which Lina was too loyal and too sensitive to admit she regretted?

What if she had let him assume it, put the interpretation in his mind? It wasn't clever to make a parade of your feeling for another man, and the girl who wore her heart on her sleeve in an office, or anywhere else, soon found she was far too good a target.

During his vacation Jimmy spent a day in Philadelphia with the cousins with whom he had made his home after his parents' death. Sam Gage had given him his first job and found him the berth with Americo. He was a good soul, steady and plodding. Both he and his wife were distressed that as yet they had not met Lina. But they'd come to town some day, and make a celebration of the occasion.

By the end of the first week Jimmy was fed up. He persuaded Lina to go away for the week-end, to a quiet little place on Long Island where they could swim and walk and play some indifferent tennis. But they had to be back Sunday night so that she could get to the office on time and without haste on Monday. And then the second week began.

During that week Kit Fawcett came on and he and Alice were married. It was an evening wedding and Lina and Jimmy went over to Brooklyn. Lina had a new and becoming frock

71

and they taxied. It was all very extravagant and rather nice. Nancy and Tad were there too, and Lina parried their reproaches. She had seen very little of Nancy since her marriage. She and Tad had come to the apartment twice — or was it three times? — but their plans to be together often hadn't materialized. You know how it is, other work, other interests, it's so easy to lose touch.

Nancy was, however, not seriously upset. What affection there was between her and her former roommate had been for the most part on her side and she knew it. She thought Lina had changed since leaving Americo, and not, she told Tad privately, for the better. She was so sure of herself, and a little hard.

They all saw Kit and Alice off in a shower of rice and confetti and long after midnight Lina and Jimmy, with Tad and Nancy sharing their taxi, were on their way across Manhattan Bridge. It was a clear still night, very warm. The water was black and slow-flowing and the stars looked down. There were scrubwomen in the Wall Street buildings, and the windows were picked out in gold. Lina drew her breath sharply. New York had the power to move her, nights like this or on clear cold days, the towers vivid against the blue. It was a superb city, it was her own. It was a pitiless town, hard and gay and brilliant. But to those who loved it, and knew it and did battle with it, it had much to offer, great rewards.

"It was such a lovely wedding," said Nancy, sighing, "and Alice looked — beautiful."

"She's very handsome," conceded Lina carelessly. Personally she had thought the wedding dull, the people stuffy, the whole atmosphere as sentimental as a moving picture. There were one or two things she must remember to tell Bea. She liked her own wedding better, the ceremony in the quiet, sedate parlor of the minister. No frills about it, no fuss. You just stood up and were married.

She put her arm through Jimmy's. "Lucky dog, you can sleep tomorrow, and I have to go off to the treadmill," she said.

Chapter Five:

NEW VISTAS

Summer seemed determined to make the most of her season. The papers found the weather convenient for headlines. *Warmest August in ten years*, they announced and appeared to take genuine pleasure in statistics of deaths by heat prostration, sunstroke, and drowning. Now and then Lina and Jimmy escaped briefly for a week-end, and were persuaded twice by Tad and Nancy to spend a day at the beaches — "with a choice between Rye and Manhattan," commented Beatrice when Lina described the horrors of these occasions. "I'll take a sidecar."

After the second outing Tad told Nancy in no uncertain tones that the next time they asked Lina and Jimmy to spend a day at the beach with them, they'd go alone. "She's a bum sport," he said definitely. "Jim's all right, but Lina's got an idea she's Mrs. Van Astorbilt or something. 'Oh, see the common people!' " he added in a falsetto, " 'aren't they too dreadful?' "

Nancy giggled. She reproached him, however, with exaggeration. "You know she didn't say that!"

"She didn't have to," replied Tad. "She looked it, down her nose. Pretty little nose too. If I were Jimmy I'd take a sock at it."

Lina had her own explanation of her behavior. She and Jimmy came close to quarreling on their return that evening.

"You might at least pretend you are having a good time," he said; "after all, it was Tad's party."

"It isn't my idea of a good time," she retorted, "millions of people, screaming babies, picnic parties. I hate crowds, Jimmy. I work hard all week, I think I'm entitled to a little rest on Sundays. I loathe being pushed around and trampled on. And I don't think that's an unreasonable reaction."

"Well, we won't go again," he said flatly; "it's hard going for me, having to cover up your disapproval. You get that we-are-not-amused look and then it's wet blankets for four."

He was tired too, wilted, cross. Lina, looking wan, despite a sunburn, shrugged and went into their bedroom. She had a way of drooping her slender shoulders and dragging her little feet that shrieked of fatigue and never failed to soften him. He followed her after a time and put his arms about her. "I'm sorry, honey; it's a silly thing to fight over — we'll go somewhere by ourselves Sundays."

She leaned her head against him and sniffed a little, pathetically. "I didn't mean to be a damper on the party, but — I hated it," she told him. "I'd rather we went out alone, somewhere, just the two of us."

Jimmy would rather too, he told her enthusiastically, putting a finger under her chin, tipping up her face and kissing her wet eyes and unsteady mouth. Yet as the summer wore on he discovered that they were not to be alone over the week-ends. On the contrary, they were almost always with other people.

Beatrice had taken a little house in Connecticut. Over the week-ends she filled it with people. A negligible cousin, elderly, deaf, and nearsighted, ran it for her and lived in it rent free, with two kittens and a police dog and a cook, during the week. Beatrice explained her to Lina.

"She embodies the conventions," she said solemnly, "the better conventions, a sort of super Mrs. Grundy — hearing practically nothing and seeing very little. She hasn't a soul in the world, and she's glad of a roof over her head. We get along divinely. I shout insults at her and she says, 'Isn't that nice, dear?'"

During September Jimmy found himself at Beatrice's every Saturday to Sunday night. Onslow came for two week-ends and Jimmy disliked him more each time he saw him. There were other men, including Beatrice's current cardiac complication, one Ralph Aldene, a tall gentleman, thin as a squirt of Vichy, with deep-set blue eyes, graying hair, and no visible means of support. He had once enjoyed a year at Oxford and for that reason insisted that he be called Rafe. This annoyed young Mr. Hall, who discovered inadvertently that Mr. Aldene's

76

birthplace was Detroit, Michigan.

Lina didn't like him. She said, tentatively, to Beatrice over a lunch table one day, "I do think you're wasting your time, Beatrice —"

Beatrice raised her eyebrows almost to her bangs. She replied without rancor, "I always do. I have a genius for falling in love with the most impossible men. But it isn't a waste of time, Lina. You'd be surprised. And I'm not planning to marry him — even if he'd have me."

Lina said, angrily, "Have you! At the drop of the handkerchief!"

"I'm not so besotted," Beatrice told her coolly, "that I don't know enough not to drop it. I also know that my salary interests Mr. Aldene more than my beautiful eyes. So I'm not having any. But meantime, I'm enjoying all the painful pleasure of unrequited love. You know that's the perfect way, really. You idiotic children who prate about the joys of mutual love don't know the half of it. The only man who fell in love with me at the time I fell in love with him was the man I married. I found I hadn't the temperament to watch the home fires burning out. I like it this way better. Rafe's disagreeable and unpleasant and eminently no good. But when he takes it into what passes for his intelligence to be sweet —" She pushed her plate away and smiled. Then she said briskly, "After a while I'll get tired of him, and no harm done."

It was difficult for Lina to follow these emotional processes. She said after a while, "But, Beatrice, what does he do — I mean, how does he earn a living?"

"He's asked out a good deal," said Beatrice, "food and drink practically free. He plays a marvelous game of auction. That's pocket money. Sometimes he rides the polo ponies of his rich friends. He does little jobs on commission. He has a flair for interior decoration, and friends in the business. He steers people their way and they pay him for it. He used to be with a champagne outfit, you know. Some day he may get another job."

Lina said slowly, "I don't see how you can respect him."

"What has that to do with it?" asked Beatrice, laughing. "Really at times, Lina, you are divinely naïve!"

Little by little Lina, and through her Jimmy, became a part of Beatrice's immediate circle. This meant going out nights, meant smoking and drinking a good deal, meant returning invitations and spending money. Lina worried over the latter aspect of their social education more than her husband did.

He said reasonably, when she complained, "But you can't go out a lot and not do something in return. Of course, most of the time it's Dutch, but even so —"

"It costs too much," said Lina.

"Then," suggested Jimmy, "let's cut 'em out. I'm willing."

She said, quickly, "But they're fun. And I like meeting new people. Interesting people. People who do things."

"People who do people you mean," asked Jimmy, "such as our distinguished friend, Rafe?"

"He's an exception. I meant writers, artists, musicians, stage people —"

Jimmy laughed. "They may be all right," he told her, "but most of 'em are a little rich for my blood. I never heard so much talk about nothing in my life."

"They talk about their work — and themselves," she contradicted.

"That's what I meant," said Jimmy gently. "None of them have amounted to much. They're all going to. Or so they say. They spend a great deal of time talking about it. I suppose it wouldn't occur to them to stop and *do* something, for a change."

"They can't all begin at the top!"

"Oh, forget 'em. Come over here. Lina, I hardly see you any more. If we aren't going out, people are coming in. It's getting to be a damned nuisance."

"Poor Jimmy." She sat on the arm of his chair and leaned down to kiss him. "Your idea of an ideal life is bread, cheese, and kisses, and love in a cottage, isn't it? With," she added, "the patter of little feet."

"Stop talking like Beatrice," he commanded. He added after a moment, "I don't like cheese — much."

He was, he conceded, sitting off in a corner in someone's studio — sometimes he didn't know whose — with an unwanted highball in one hand — getting to be a grouch. But the summer had been difficult. He had driven the little Americo car through his big district day after day, his hat pushed back on his forehead, his collar loosened, stifled with heat, with gas, with traffic. People went haywire in the heat. They drove like mad. He'd had one or two near-accidents. And he'd worked hard and come home at night, half dead, to find Lina had accepted an invitation or was herself too tired to cook, and would he run around to the delicatessen, or would they get a bite at some teashop or other?

He hated teashops. His legs were too long, there was never room at the table. And as for delicatessen food — he liked it enormously, for snacks, late suppers, on occasions and picnics, but when it came to night after night — he rebelled.

In addition to his regular work he was keeping what amounted to a notebook of Jelly Joy. This was for Lina. She was still insistent that the one-meal-to-a-flavor package would be a real addition to Americo's sales. Anything she could learn in support of her argument would be that much to the good. So Jimmy found himself interviewing housewives who came into the shop to buy their supplies, and asking them what they would think of such an innovation.

When in the late autumn Lina had an imposing array of facts and figures assembled, she went out to lunch with Onslow. She had not spoken to him of her brain wave but now she did so, leaning across the table, jotting down figures on a menu, eager, animated and very pretty. He told her so.

"It's a mistake for any woman as lovely as you are to be in business — and married."

"That's sweet of you," said Lina cordially. "Look here, George, I spoke of this while I was still with Americo. I didn't get far with it. But I thought if I could interest someone in the agency — someone important, someone who would have influence. . . . After all, they're planning a new package. They might as well plan two while they're at it. I could turn out some awfully good copy. You know, advice for brides, that sort of thing."

Onslow frowned, his dark, attractive face intent. Finally he asked, "How well do you know Lowell?"

Lowell was the vice-president. He was a close personal friend of Americo's president. It was through Lowell that the account had come to the agency.

"I don't know him at all," answered Lina mournfully.

"Well," said Onslow, "I'll give you a tip. He's a pretty hard nut to crack. Shaw's the hailfellow, Harcourt's the financial expert, Lowell's the rest of the works. Comparatively blue nose.

He's the one who makes 'em refuse accounts he doesn't like. Turned down half a million in some patent baby food two years ago because it didn't come up to his standards. Dislikes women in the advertising game; accepts them now as a necessary evil, because they probably know something about consumer appeal from the woman's angle. Has a daughter about your age. Likes giving advice. He has the final word over the copy, you know. I don't get to him often. Howard does, of course."

Lina nodded. She remarked, after a moment, "This lobster thermidor is marvelous."

Onslow threw back his head and laughed. He said appreciatively, "So are you."

A week later Lina was working overtime. It wasn't necessary. Of course, a good many of the copy writers did work overtime, especially when a campaign was in the making. As it happened there was no great rush for her present copy, the fourth or fifth advertisement in the Jelly Joy campaign which would start after the New Year. But she worked overtime just the same, a green shade over her eyes and her door open. Beatrice looked in on her before quitting. "What's the big idea?" she inquired.

"Work."

"There's more in this than meets the eye," Beatrice surmised. "You look very appealing in there, busy as a little bee — what's the sting in it? And the eyeshade is becoming. Have you phoned Jimmy?"

"I have," said Lina demurely.

"Well," said Beatrice, "I can't see anything up your sleeve but don't tell me. Is George working overtime tonight, too?"

"He is not!" Lina replied with spirit.

Mr. Lowell was. She had heard him barking an order at his secretary when she passed his door in the late afternoon. Howard, the copy chief, and one of the other partners were having a conference with him, after hours. Coffee and sandwiches would be sent in. No telephone messages. They were not to be disturbed.

At six-thirty Lina left the office and went downstairs and around to Madison Avenue to a drugstore. She came back with a bottle of milk and a sandwich, and went to work again. She left her door open. Howard, returning from his office with something from the files, looked in and saw her.

"Struck a snag?" he inquired.

"No," she replied, and smiled up at him, "just had a bright idea, that's all, and was afraid I'd lose it before morning."

Mr. Lowell, tall, heavily paunched, was at the door of his own office looking impatiently for Howard. When Howard reached him, "Who's that?" he asked.

"Miss Lawrence," said Howard, the convention of the maiden name having been established. "She's working late on some of the Jelly Joy copy."

"Oh," Lowell frowned. He said presently,

"She's doing well, isn't she? I like her stuff."

"She's very clever," said Howard.

"We might have her in later," said Lowell, "as she happens to be here."

At nine o'clock Lina was summoned. She had been writing letters for the last hour. She swept them into her drawer, snapped it shut, picked up a notebook and followed Howard to the office of the vice-president. "What on earth —" she began. "I'm scared to death."

"Don't be," said Howard. "He just wants to ask you a question or two. It wouldn't have occurred to him if you hadn't been here." His head ached and he was beginning to feel the need of a drink.

Lina walked into the office ahead of him and looked in frightened appeal at Mr. Lowell. Mr. Shaw, who had an eye for blondes and had noticed her more than once, smiled at her encouragingly.

Lowell messed up the papers on his desk and barked at her. His weary and browbeaten secretary sighed and settled back in her chair. Perhaps Lina Lawrence could take it. She was beginning to feel that she couldn't.

"Sit down, Miss — Miss —" began Lowell. Shaw, Howard, and the secretary supplied the name in one breath. "Lawrence," said Lowell, glaring, "I was perfectly aware of it."

He had her most recent copy for Jelly Joy on the desk. He pawed at it a moment, spread it out before her. "There's one little matter," he said. "Howard doesn't agree with me on it. I think you've overemphasized —"

Shaw interrupted. "If you're through with me, Pete," he said.

"Run along," said Lowell, "and you too, Fred. We've finished. I just wanted to ask Miss Lawrence —" He turned to his secretary. "Meantime, you can get all the Jelly Joy data for me, if you will."

Presently Lina was alone with him in the enormous paneled office, with its clipper ship prints and five windows, the soft red draperies pulled across them. She confessed, looking at the sentence he had marked, "I wasn't quite satisfied with that. But Mr. Howard seemed to think it all right." She looked at the big man frankly. "And I think he's right. It — it was just that it isn't worded as I'd have it. If you could advise me . . ."

She was small, and young, and fair. Nothing stridently modern about her. He disliked Beatrice Harris very much, and suffered her because he knew that she was brilliant. But he hated her too-bright mouth and her too-expensive clothes and her hard air of studied poise. This girl was different. She was wholly feminine. He observed with approval that she was not made up, nor was she saturated with cigarette smoke.

Ten minutes later when his secretary returned with the folder she found them laughing together and talking quite like old friends. She raised a weary eyebrow, paid a silent tribute, and received her dismissal for the evening.

Lina rose, presently. She said gratefully, "You've taught me more about copy writing in the last ten minutes than I'd learned in six months."

He smiled amiably at her. "You remind me of my daughter," he said, and his face softened; "she knows how to flatter the old man too."

"She's very lucky," said Lina, "I never knew my father. . . . I wasn't flattering you, Mr. Lowell."

He believed her. She was an honest little thing, he thought. He asked, "How long have you been with us?"

"Since the first of June."

"Oh, of course. Came direct from Americo. You know a lot about this product. It's been a problem," he admitted, frowning. "The competition is enormous. It hasn't moved the way it should."

She said, standing there, "I — I have an idea for a new package. You see, I was present at one conference with the agency while I was still at Americo. You weren't there. You were out of town. Mr. Shaw came. . . . I told them — but — well, perhaps it wasn't very sensible but somehow I think —"

"Suppose you tell me," he suggested.

Shortly after ten-thirty the Lowell car dropped Lina at her apartment. She went up in the self-operating elevator and Jimmy opened the flat door to her before she could ring.

"What's the big idea?" he demanded. "I've been nearly nuts. Have you any idea of the time?"

She wasn't listening. "Jimmy," she cried, "I've put it over."

"What?"

"The one-meal package. At least I think I have. I've been talking to Mr. Lowell about it; he brought me home, by the way — he's a grand old person — and he thinks there's something to it. He's going to take it up with Americo. I'm to plan the campaign for it — do the copy — if it goes over. He — he didn't say anything — but it may mean a raise, Jimmy." She rushed at him, kissed him. Then she said, "I'm starved. I could eat a couple of wolves. What's in the icebox?"

Chapter Six:

UNDERTOW

Lina kept her counsel. She said nothing at the agency, neither to Beatrice nor to George Onslow nor to Pete Howard, of her talk with Mr. Lowell. Time enough for them to know when the issue was settled, and if during the next few weeks she was called rather often to the account executive's office, she offered no explanation.

Beatrice, of course, had a word to say.

"All," she uttered, "is not on the up and up in Denmark. You are plotting something, my little petunia. Out with it. Tell Auntie."

Lina widened her eyes.

"No," said Beatrice firmly, "don't do that. It's completely wasted. Try it on your piano, or upon Messrs. Jimmy, George, or whom-have-you. You are up to something, my girl. The well-known game of tit-tat-toe which," she added casually, "is more than likely to become the double cross. You and Jimmy skid over to the apartment tonight. I've added to my collection."

Beatrice collected porcelain, first editions, perfumes — and men. The new addition proved to be a youngish actor, authentically British and almost offensively attractive. Rafe, apparently, had served his purpose and was no more.

The apartment was extremely chic and without charm. The furniture was steel and leather, wood and fur, glass and chromium. The etchings were good. "After all," exclaimed Beatrice, "in these days a girl must have etchings — too." There was a small, complete bar, a magnificent phonograph — Beatrice could not endure the radio — gardenias in silver bowls, and a color scheme that was white and scarlet in the living-room, black and white and heaven blue in the bedroom, and yellow and green in the bathroom. The kitchen was all white, severely surgical.

The place gave Jimmy the creeps. Lina adored it. It was, she said, madly sophisticated. But her adoration did not prevent her agreeing with George Onslow when he said uneasily that, after all, he preferred a place which did not look like a decorator's nightmare. His idea of a home was a little spot in the country, hedges, roses, overstuffed furniture, dogs, books.

"Of course," approved Lina quickly. They were sitting together on Beatrice's unfathomable divan, the scarlet one. "I quite agree. Poor Beatrice." She leveled her clear gray regard on Onslow and asked, after a moment, "But this apartment expresses her, don't you think — hard and brilliant, and — frustrated?"

Onslow was impressed. In addition to being feminine and lovely, Lina was clever, and sound psychologically. He envied Jimmy. He could not know that Beatrice, having no illusions about anything, including herself, had remarked, the first time Lina came to the apartment, "I call it Frustration Flats . . . looks like I feel."

Christmas came and went. It wasn't the Christmas Jimmy had planned. He remembered others, at home, on Chestnut Hill. A tall tree and the smell of pine, the shiny crimson of holly, the unwinding lengths of colored ribbon, laughter, and the fragrance of good cooking, tissue paper crackling, and somewhere, chimes.

He went shopping for Lina. He bought her perfume and lingerie, and a wrist watch that he knew he couldn't afford, which was why he bought it. Christmas isn't any fun unless you dive off the springboard of common sense into the waters of extravagance. He went to the five-and-ten and selected absurdities for her stocking. He wanted to buy her a wire-haired terrier but he knew that she didn't care for dogs and that a dog might not be the most sensible addition to their home life. It was selfishness to consider it. It was he who wanted it, not Lina.

On Christmas Eve he came home late, his arms full of packages, holly and a small tree. Lina was there before him, at the telephone. She hung up as he came in.

"Lucky you left the door open," he said cheerfully. "Hey, catch — and go easy with this one. It's tree trimming."

"Jimmy! For heaven's sake!" Lina looked

with dismay at the general litter.

"Tonight," he told her, "we'll trim it. Nice little tree, isn't it? And hang up stockings. And listen to the radio. Did you ask Nan and Tad over for dinner tomorrow?"

"They're going to his people," she answered. "I —" she regarded him with an abashed glance that made her look very young — "I'm not equal to cooking a turkey, so it's just as well. I canceled the order."

"You what?"

"Canceled it," she explained patiently. "I thought we could sleep late and go out for lunch. Beatrice just called up. She's decided to throw a party."

"But," he said, "Christmas is for home!"

He was, she saw instantly, hurt. She did not want to hurt him. She was still very much in love with him, too much sometimes for her own peace of mind, the singleness of her purpose. She went over and inserted herself deftly in his arms as he stood staring at her blankly.

"But we'll have all day," she said softly. "Jimmy, I didn't know you felt this way. I've never paid much attention to Christmas. It wasn't any fun, up home. And, of course, since I came to New York it's been just another holiday to get through somehow. Nancy used to go home, when she could. She always asked me, but I hadn't any right to intrude, so I stayed here and pretended it was like any day."

She had always the power to move him. He

thought of her in pictures. Little lonely kid, face against the pastry-shop window. Watching the festivities from the outside, hearing the carols. You couldn't appreciate what you'd never had, couldn't understand something you'd never known.

She said swiftly, "Don't be disappointed, darling. I promised Beatrice. But we'll trim the tree and hang up the stockings. I'm afraid I haven't very much for yours. Next year it will be different," she promised.

Ties, socks, and for his special present a handsome, expensive lighter. She'd bought them recently during a lunch hour, without much thought. Just one of the things one did, that was all. For a Good Husband.

They trimmed the tree, which seemed small and tawdry to Jimmy after it was over, and they stood back and looked at it. He was seeing it through her eyes now. They hung the holly wreaths and Lina's stocking. They listened to the radio until Lina yawned and said, over her shoulder, "I'm going to bed — turn that thing off, will you?"

But it was twelve o'clock. Jimmy did not switch the dials until the chimes had ceased their silver message. Then he followed her into the bedroom and took her in his arms. "Merry Christmas, darling," he said gently. "Our first — may there be many more."

On the following night they were at Beatrice's with twenty or more people. There was a good deal to eat and drink and Beatrice had a funny stiff tree of painted wood hung with absurd and sometimes embarrassing gifts. She had very modern angels for trimming, and there was considerable laughter when her actor — who was "resting" — appeared as Santa Claus, to distribute the gifts, with the most amusing comments. He was, everyone agreed, perfectly killing, and the most realistic drunk they'd ever seen. And when it came to his remarks on the dear little children of the world who, it appeared, had driven him to drink — well, he was a scream — and shouldn't someone call him to the attention of the big producers? A blackout Santa should be too too divine.

Everyone except Jimmy had a marvelous time. He laughed a good deal and drank slightly too much, because he was so bored, and a little melancholy. He was suddenly not so resentful of these friends of Lina's as he was sorry for them. They didn't know anything that mattered. If this was their idea of Christmas, well, heaven help them. Not that they believed in heaven. The rye gave him a brief clarity of thought, and vision, and he regarded them, milling about the room, laughing, screaming, doing mock reverence to the cockeyed angels, with genuine pity. Shallow, driven, afraid, clever in an age habituated to cleverness, terrified of sentiment, of the cliché, of the trite and the true — more completely understanding the mind and the body than any other generation,

the vagaries of one, the needs of the other —
and more completely blind to the spirit.

"Didn't we have a grand time?" sighed Lina,
in the taxi going home. She leaned her heavy
head against his shoulder. It had been such fun.
Beatrice's friends accepted her as one of them.
They called her by her Christian name, they
confided in her, flirted with her, according to
their sex — and were amused by her, pleased
with her appearance, her mental agility.

"Sure," said Jimmy, "it was swell."

If that was her definition of happiness — But
it wasn't, not really, he assured himself, as she
drowsed against him. She only thought it was.
She'd learn, in time, by degrees. He couldn't
force his opinions on her, he couldn't make her
over, all at once. She'd been seduced into be-
lieving that Beatrice's way of life was the only
way. He didn't dislike Beatrice. She entertained
him vastly, often. But she had no importance,
no significance. Some day Lina would come to
see that. Nor was Beatrice, he realized, loyal to
anyone or anything, even to herself.

He was no prig. Beatrice had invited him to
kiss her tonight — under the mistletoe which
hung over the bar. He had done so with alacrity
and had enjoyed it — in the spirit in which the
invitation was given. Lina hadn't seen, and it
was not essential that he mention it. In
Beatrice's crowd people kissed freely, and no
harm done. Well, he liked Beatrice, but a steady
diet of that exotic fare would have ruined his

appetite not alone for simpler nourishment, but for any at all. If only Lina would keep her head and understand that Beatrice wasn't the last word on any subject, and enjoy her for what she was worth — which was very little!

On the following day the agency was closed, and it was just as well, for Lina was ill, ill enough to demand Jimmy's full attention. He took care of her, consoled her, laughed at her when she would not admit that she'd had too much party. "You'll be telling me next that it was something you ate!" he said.

By evening she had recovered sufficiently to eat the scrambled eggs and thin toast, and to drink the tea he brought her. She stretched out on the old bed-divan in the living-room and ate with him from a tray. And was sweet and languid, and dependent on him.

"You're a darling," she said, as he stooped to take the tray away.

He thought, carrying it to the kitchen, that it was better than being a sap. He'd overheard George Onslow: "Who is he? Oh, that's Lina Lawrence's husband. No, his name's Hall. Nice fellow — if something of a sap. Why she ever —"

It still rankled.

Long after she slept that night he lay there thinking. If things had been different. If his parents had not been killed in the accident. If he had been able to go to Princeton as they had planned — if he had been equipped for the profession he'd chosen, that of engineering? So what? So he would have never become an Americo employee, and would have never met Lina. Surely she was worth all the universities in the world?

The New Year came. It was an electric New Year, tingling with hope, with promise. An election had come and gone. In March there would be an inauguration. And the people of the United States, on that New Year, looked upward, as children look, and perceived a new beauty on the horizon, an iridescent beauty, like that of a vast, breath-taking bubble, rising swiftly and surely. And as they had blown it themselves, they admired it very much.

During that January Lina was informed that Jelly Joy, through Americo, had considered her proposal of the one-meal-to-a-flavor package and were going to manufacture it. She would have full charge of the special campaign for the new package, under Mr. Howard's direction, and a raise in salary. Business, Mr. Lowell said confidentially, was bound to improve now. Prosperity was a step nearer the corner. Advertisers would be willing to spend more money, and the consumer public would follow the advertisers. Miss Lawrence would have her salary doubled. The agency believed in its young people. They went up by merit. They had every opportunity to go up fast and far. He congratulated her.

"So that was what you had up the sleeve," said Beatrice. "I wish I'd thought of it myself.

This calls for a celebration at Twenty-One, after hours."

Onslow, hearing, beamed at her. "I knew you'd put it over," he said.

"I hope I can," she told him. "I'm a little scared. I'll probably make a nuisance of myself, asking for advice."

She did not intend to; she could get along nicely by herself, thank you, and thanks, too, to Jimmy's information. But men had funny ideas about women's success. And a hundred-per-cent raise in salary was success, wasn't it? So it behooved her to disarm Mr. Onslow. In this, too, she succeeded.

Mr. Lowell thought of her as his discovery. And Mr. Onslow thought of her as a fair, deserving creature whom he'd assisted with the right word at the right time. Which harmed neither of them as neither confided in the other.

"I really owe it to you, Beatrice," said Lina over a table at 21. "If you hadn't given me self-confidence, I wouldn't have dared."

"Save that for the superior sex," advised Beatrice lazily. "As if I didn't read you like Sanskrit." But as she raised her glass and said, "Here's mud in your eye," she felt a warmer glow than the cocktail afforded. After all, she had bucked the kid up, when she needed it. *My one good deed*, she thought, astonished; *if I don't look out I'll be joining the Scouts.*

Lina looked at her new wrist watch.

"I must fly. Jimmy'll be fit to be tied."

"He is tied," said Beatrice, "hogtied. How's he going to take this?"

"How should he take it?" asked Lina. "He'll be delighted, of course. Jimmy's *grand!*"

"I don't dispute that, my proud beauty. But — you're making more than he is, aren't you?"

"Well, yes."

"Break it to him gently," suggested Beatrice. "Men are funny that way."

"Jimmy isn't selfish,"cried Lina indignantly.

"He won't call it that," prophesied Beatrice, "whatever you or I may think. Take a tip from one who has lain on the sawmill as the train came rushing on. Or was it the track? I forget. Soft pedal your raise."

Lina did not need that advice, although it caused her, perhaps, to rearrange the order in which her news was imparted. The important thing she stressed was that "their" idea had gone over. She told Jimmy so over and over. "If it hadn't been for you, darling." Of course, she reflected, that was true, in a way. Still, she thought further, flushed with victory more than with the refreshment in the oasis of 21, even without Jimmy's help I would have worked it out. It was simply a short cut. But give the devil his due, she decided generously. Not that Jimmy was a devil.

She tossed in the raise, as it were, carelessly.

Jimmy whistled when he heard it. He said, after a minute, "I'm tickled to death for you, Lina —"

"For us," she corrected gravely, sweetly.

"No, for you. It's what you wanted. But —"

"Jimmy — don't say it! Don't let money make any difference. How can it? It's yours as much as mine. What do we care who earns it?" she asked him intensely. She flung herself into his arms, kissed him, laid her cheek against his own. "Darling, we'll have so much fun."

He said, in a stifled voice, "I'll have to work harder than ever — for that district manager-ship."

"You'll get it," she promised him as if she spoke for Americo, and as one promises a toy to a child, "and — soon."

"Then," he said soberly, "you'll quit? I know it will be asking a lot, Lina. More than when you first promised. But you did promise."

"Of course, I'll quit," she said soothingly, al-most mechanically. She smoothed out the frown between his eyes with her fingertips. "That's better. Jimmy, couldn't we have a car? Just a small one? It would be just what we need. I'm terrified of taxis. And we can afford it — now."

They could, he supposed, with their com-bined incomes; they could afford a small car, a better apartment. But —

He said hesitantly, "Lina, if you'd save — the whole increase? So you'd have something. You could invest it, after a while, in government bonds. I'd feel so much safer for you. And if we live up to all of this, then when the time comes and I get the raise I'll be asking you to live on about half. If you get accustomed to the other way, you'll hate it —"

She said, "I intend to save. But really, Jimmy — a little car? It wouldn't cost much to run. I've earned it," she told him.

That was the beginning . . . a little car, a bargain silver fox, a divan for the living-room, new draperies made by the "little man" whom Beatrice recommended and who proved so expensive. Jimmy became aware that Lina had little if any intention of saving more money than before her increase. He learned also that, if it was something she wanted, it was "our" money when she announced her intention; but that it was "my" money if he disapproved. And he learned further that one hundred dollars a week was chicken feed. It wouldn't be long now, a year at the most, before she'd be earning double that: if the campaign went over, if the new package caught on, if the sales came up —

He had plenty of time to think over the situation. He contracted flu and was very ill, so ill that Lina remained away from the office for a day, and hovered over him incompetently. She was terrified and it was a pity that he was too ill to know or care — shaking with chill, burning with fever, feeling like nothing on earth. Beatrice, appealed to, sent her own doctor, a personable and clever young man as Beatrice's doctor would be. He drove east from Park Avenue, with a gardenia in his buttonhole, and after his examination told Lina that Jimmy was a pretty sick lad and would need careful nursing.

She said, quite honestly, yet fully aware that she struck the right note, "But I'm so stupid, Dr. Drake. I'm a very bad nurse. I don't know anything about nursing. I'm all thumbs. And then, I'm so *scared*."

He said consolingly, "It isn't stupidity, it's quite natural. You've probably had very little to do with illness and not all women have the flair."

Personally he preferred those who didn't. He hadn't fallen in love with more than one nurse in his life and that had been during the salad days of his internship. He dealt with illness every day, and with nurses. He had reached the point where he preferred women pretty and inefficient — women, that is, whose business was not the care of the sick.

He suggested, "I could send a very capable nurse who will do twenty-four-hour duty. She's the last of the old guard. Could you manage . . . ?"

He looked around the little apartment, and added:

"He won't need expert care at night for very long, we'll hope. After that he can get along with a day nurse. The convalescent care is important in this disease."

"I'll manage," said Lina eagerly.

The nurse came. She was fifty, and Scotch.

Lina arranged for her to sleep on the divan, within call. She arranged for a maid who would come before breakfast and leave after dinner. She had intended to install one anyway during the spring. If the girl worked out, they'd keep her on. And she herself went to Beatrice's apartment during the week Mrs. Campbell remained on twenty-four-hour duty.

Mrs. Campbell didn't approve of wives who moved out when nurses moved in. But Lina, coming every day, before and after her work, explained.

"I have to keep my job," she said. "Oh, Mrs. Campbell, I'm so terribly grateful to you."

So that was it, thought Mrs. Campbell commiseratingly. She liked her patient. He was docile, boyishly embarrassed, and as he grew better, attractive. It probably wasn't his fault that this pretty girl had to support him. Nowadays the best of men were out of jobs. She thought of Campbell, whose fault it had been that she'd had to work her fingers to the bone. But Jimmy Hall wasn't at all like Campbell, and she was sorry for him and for his little wife.

It wasn't until Jimmy was on the road to recovery, having narrowly escaped pneumonia, that Mrs. Campbell learned that he had a job of his own. She tried to revise her opinion of Lina, to turn pity into disapproval — these modern young things! — but couldn't, quite. Lina had got under her skin. And you couldn't say she wasn't in love with her husband. Mrs.

Campbell recognized love when she saw it.

Lina moved back to the living-room divan, and Mrs. Campbell came daytimes. But it was over two weeks before Dr. Drake believed it safe to dismiss her entirely and another week before Jimmy went back to work. He was by that time a very impatient young man, loathing his own weakness, his fatigue, his normal petulance. He snapped at Lina and he snapped at the new maid who, it appeared, was staying on. He demanded in no uncertain terms what all this was costing him: Park Avenue medicos, trained nurses, servants . . .

"But now that you're all right," said Lina, "Kate will come only part time. To clean and get dinner. That is, after you return to work."

He said flatly, "I can't afford it."

"We can," Lina corrected him.

She had been extremely unhappy during his illness. Staying with Beatrice hadn't been any fun at all. She lay awake nights wondering if the phone would ring, dreading it. Suppose anything were to happen? But it couldn't; Jimmy was young, strong. Nothing could happen. Yet you read, every day in the papers, of men as young, as strong as he . . .

Now he was well again and she forgot how frightened she had been.

"I'm paying my own bills," he said sulkily, "and if you must have this woman — though for what, heaven knows — I'll pay her too."

He paid the rent, the gas, the electricity, the

food. He could cut down on other things, lunches, tobacco. If he couldn't run his own house he'd have no self-respect. He'd manage the maid too. Lina could spend her money on clothes and furs and cars. He didn't care. But this was his job.

Lina said, "You needn't take my head off!"

It was the beginning: of bickering over trivial things, of quarreling over money, of tears and reconciliations, and even in their more composed relations, of a continuous undercurrent, swift below the surface, and deep, undermining the foundations of the marriage they were building.

Chapter Seven:

CAMPAIGN WITHOUT BANNERS

March was distinguished by an inauguration, a sounding of cymbals, symbols, and silver tongues throughout the land, and other phenomena. In common with the majority of citizens, politics interested Lina only in so far as they affected her personally. Imbued with the happy thought of Bigger and Better Business, talking in capitals as a preparation to re-learning the alphabet, she concentrated on the Jelly Joy campaign to the exclusion of almost every other interest.

After less than a year in the advertising agency, she had picked up the jargon to an astonishing degree. Jimmy found this amusing at first, then boring, and finally irritating.

In May Tad and Nancy were married and upon their return from a brief honeymoon Lina asked them to dinner. She and Jimmy had, of course, not attended the wedding in South Bend. Lina had sent an expensive gift in their name and Nancy called her at the office on her return.

"We're living," Nancy informed her, "in a flat on Washington Heights, in which almost everything disappears. You just push buttons. It's lots of fun. Look, Lina, I hate to ask this — but may I change your present? It's perfectly swell and gorgeously beautiful, but we need every inch of space we have and even a coffee table takes up too much room. I thought — you see, we need china."

Lina said, "Of course," and a little later in the conversation set the date for dinner. Telling Jimmy of it that night, she ignored his comment, "It's about time we saw 'em again," and went on, "Of all the idiotic things! Why couldn't they wait? After all, in these times, especially as Nancy has given up her job!"

Jimmy said, after a moment, "Nancy's where she wants to be. In a place of her own — with Tad. And times," he commented, grinning, "are going to improve. You've said so, yourself."

Lina frowned slightly. She replied, after a minute, "I know, but — there's no sense in taking chances. And speaking of taking chances —" She crossed the room to sit on the arm of his chair, leaning against him. "I was thinking — every little bit would help Tad, and you really should increase your insurance."

"I can't afford it," said Jimmy shortly.

Lina had her little car. She had the now indispensable Kate, who was neat and quick and a good cook. The small establishment ran smoothly. And if Jimmy sat up nights struggling over budgets and checkbooks, if Jimmy grew leaner and less talkative, if he didn't sleep well and if he had acquired a certain type of nervous indigestion which caused him to regard his morning coffee with distaste, whose fault was it?

His, of course, and his male stubbornness. If only he'd let her do more with her money and stop fussing, Lina wailed at him time and time again. But the upkeep of their living expenses devolved on him, he assured her. No argument could move him.

Lina suggested tentatively, "Jimmy, I could carry the extra premium."

"No," said Jimmy.

She said, "It seems to me you're being very selfish. I don't like to talk about this any more than you do. But if anything happened to you —"

"You'll get along," Jimmy told her briefly.

He regarded her, there in the quiet and friendly room, her small, charming face close to his, with something very like hostility. He regarded her with love also, for it is possible to love a woman, become her enemy, and yet not cease to love her. He was finding this out, painfully and by degrees.

"Oh," said Lina angrily, "you're impossible!"

She left him and wandered across the room, picking up a book, putting it down, turning the dials of the radio, snapping them off. Presently she said, "Let's go to a movie or have the car sent around and drive up Riverside —"

Jimmy sighed. "Can't you stay at home one evening alone with me, Lina? I'm tired."

"I'm tired too," she flung at him. "If you think it's all plain sailing — with the production department camping on the phone all day, dragging me into their constant battle with printers and presses and engravers, fussing with the bookkeeping department on charges and not getting anywhere. And if you think anyone can hurry the art department. Beatrice said today that their common state of being is one of injured arrogance. They can't be rushed. I suppose being Art for Art's sake they are superior to the rest of us. I was talking to Lem Carter only yesterday. Told me he had ideas far better than the mogul's. But when I asked him to help me out, do you think he'd bother? On the other hand, I've learned that if I don't beg advice from them the whole outfit's insulted!"

She flung herself into a chair, lit a cigarette and smoked moodily.

Jimmy said, after a while, "Aren't you smoking a lot? You didn't smoke at all — last year."

She stubbed out the cigarette. "I don't know why I do," she said frankly, "I don't like it. It hurts my throat and stains my fingers. Only everyone does at the office."

"Forget the office, can't you?" he asked her wearily.

But she wasn't listening.

"The campaign starts next month," she said. "I'm worried. If things don't go right — They must go right! It's been planned so carefully. The research department has done a good job, considering that they didn't have half the normal amount of time; scout and field men worked their heads off; there's been a house-to-house job and direct mail questionnaires . . ."

"Don't I know it?" he said, without enthusiasm. He'd done his share. Not for Americo, which had not commissioned him to do so, but for Lina. Had talked Jelly Joy to retail grocers and to customers, until he was hoarse, kept full notes — for Lina.

"Everybody," said Lina gloomily, "passes the buck to someone else. If they aren't howling at me for copy, they're yelling where the hell are the plates and mats anyway. The office staff claims it's behind because it has to do a million and one things which aren't any of its business — always working overtime because production has fallen down or something. It's a madhouse. Even the office boys are out on someone else's errand when you want 'em. The senior boss buzzes in and out — on his way back from Florida or en route to Hot Springs. The junior bosses tear their hair. As for the account executives — between the devil of clients and the deep sea of production —"

"Let's go to the movies," said Jimmy abruptly. "I'm not as tired as I thought I was."

He was, he concluded, watching the picture flicker on the screen, completely fed up with the advertising agency. Lina ate and drank and slept it — and perforce he had to as well. He had his own job to do. He was doing it well. He was showing results of which his good-natured predecessor, happily married, pleasantly situated in an office job, had never dreamed. But he didn't bring his day's work home with him — except in so far as it interested Lina. She demanded to know every last item of his daily round which might have some bearing on her own work. Otherwise she showed little, if any, interest.

Nancy and Tad came to dinner, carefree as kittens and merry as grigs. Nancy was impressed with Kate, her uniformed efficiency and her masterly way with a mixed grill. After dinner she disappeared into the kitchen to procure the recipe for escalloped tomatoes and returned with a look of smug satisfaction on her face and the announcement that Tad loved tomatoes.

Tad and Jimmy were deep in a discussion of insurance. Tad was wholly optimistic. People, he declared, who had been twice bitten, not to say macerated, in the stock market, were turning more to insurance as an investment. Of course, he admitted sadly, that didn't mean — as yet — any great volume of business. But it would; it was bound to. At the moment the borrowing on policies was pretty heavy.

"I've been trying to persuade Jimmy to take out more," said Lina casually.

Her tone was free from reproach but the implication was there. Tad, as an insurance agent, and Nancy, as his dutiful bride, regarded their host with astonishment and censure.

"If you'd let me talk to you," began Tad.

Jimmy held up a protesting hand. "There's

nothing I'd like better. But, frankly, it would be wasting your time at present, Tad. I can't afford it."

The slight impediment in Tad's speech became more marked as he argued earnestly, "You owe it to yourself and to Lina to afford it, Jimmy. You could cut down on other things —"

His glance included the new cellarette which Lina had bought recently, the larger radio, and Kate's black poplin figure deftly removing the last of the table service from the dining end of the living-room.

Jimmy shrugged. He said, "In a few years I'll come into the legacy my parents left me — insurance, by the way. A lump sum. Then we'll talk about signing on the dotted line. I had planned to put the greater part of it into an annuity for Lina."

"That's the stuff," said Tad heartily.

"How's Americo doing without me?" asked Nancy lazily, curled up on the couch, her worshipful gaze directed in the general direction of her husband.

"Just barely struggling through," Jimmy told her.

"Hear from Kit and Alice?"

"Now and then; they seem very happy."

"Alice," announced Lina, "is completely domesticated. But then she always was. And she's going to have a baby."

"Well, I'll be a so-and-so!" said Jimmy enthusiastically. "That's swell. You didn't tell me," he accused her.

"I forgot," said Lina. "It didn't seem awfully important. Besides, it's a long way off. Almost anything can happen."

"Don't say that," cried Nancy, knocking furiously on wood. "It's just whistling for bad luck."

Lina gave her a tolerant, superior smile. She said, "It's bad luck any way you look at it. They've only been married since August."

Jimmy said doggedly, "Just the same, I bet they're tickled to death."

"Alice says so," reported Lina indifferently; "of course, in their case it's different. A secure job, a home. They're living with Kit's mother and she's building them a house near by," she explained to Nancy.

"Lucky," sighed Nancy, "and the rest of us wondering not only if the roof will leak but if there'll *be* a roof tomorrow."

"Crazy kids," said Lina indulgently. "Why didn't you wait?"

Nancy looked at Tad; Tad looked at Nancy. Jimmy, intercepting that glance, looked away. After a moment Tad said, stammering earnestly:

"Well, you see, Lina, this being engaged forever business isn't so good. We were getting on each other's nerves. And as for waiting till it was economically safe and sound and respectable to get married, we decided it was no go.

We couldn't set a date, even approximately. We couldn't say: in a year, two years, five. We didn't know. So we decided that we'd rather starve together than eat, at intervals, apart. And here we are."

Jimmy applauded mildly. "Them's my sentiments."

"They would be," said Lina. "You're so impractical. Look, Nancy, come downtown and lunch with me and Beatrice Harris sometime. You liked her when you met her here, didn't you?"

"Mm, yes," replied Nancy a little dubiously. "She scares me to death and she's so darned smart she makes me feel as if I were wearing a little red shawl and carrying a basket lunch into the Ritz. Otherwise, I liked her all right."

"She's a scream," said Lina, "you ought to have heard her today on the subject of the Rate'n' Dater."

"What on earth's that?" asked Nancy, wide-eyed.

Lina explained, at length, the Standard Rate and Data — bible of the advertising agencies — and its functions. From that she went on to other things. She was off, and in good form. After a time Jimmy stopped fidgeting and relaxed over a pipe. And Lina carried on, her clear voice dominating the room.

Jimmy closed his eyes. He thought, *I have married a woman who is beautiful and clever.* He opened his eyes and looked at Nancy. Nancy

113

wasn't beautiful and she wasn't clever. Yet she wasn't dumb by a long shot, although he was well aware that Lina believed she was. Nancy was — comfortable. Nancy was silly and feminine and domestic, she was fiercely loyal, blindly trusting and very much in love. He thought, *Not that I'd exchange one Lina for a dozen Nancies — but I wonder if Tad knows how lucky he is. Or if Kit knows how lucky he is too?*

On the next day Lina, together with the rest of her department, attended the daily conference or showdown of the assorted departments, after which she and Beatrice lunched together and aired the various complaints they had omitted to air during the session. George Onslow, strolling by their table in the restaurant they affected, sat down, ordered, and made himself at home.

"I'm scared," Lina told him presently.

"Of what?" inquired George. "Surely not of me. I don't eat little girls. I merely pay their luncheon checks."

"We get going in April," she reminded him.

"And by the middle of June," prophesied George, "all the pretty little brides will be ordering the one-meal-to-a-flavor package of their favorite dessert and their husbands will be inquiring, 'Can't you make crêpes Suzette?' By the way, I heard a little rumor recently. If this goes over, Americo is thinking of putting Jelly Joy on the air in the fall."

Lina's eyes were big and bright. She said, "I wonder if I —"

"The radio department's a jealous outfit," George reminded her.

"That makes it so different from any other department," Beatrice told him languidly.

"I know," said Lina.

On the way back to the office Beatrice linked her arm through her friend's. She said, "You may be as stained glass, angel, obscurity and all to others, but to me you come wrapped in gauze, darling. What's on your mind?"

"Lunch," Lina answered. "I ate too much."

"Is that where your mind is situated?" inquired Beatrice. "I believed it a male prerogative."

Lina went back to her desk and to her routine work. She thought, looking over the rough sketches the art department had sent her and which dealt with the regular Jelly Joy advertising, *There's Malkin in the radio department. No, he wouldn't do. Too old and not old enough. There's Harry Galleon. I wonder . . .*

Of course, she reflected further, *I don't know who'd be in charge of the Jelly Joy program. But Galleon has several Americo programs now . . .*

Galleon was young. He was overworked, irritable, nervous, something of a genius, not badlooking and wholly wedded to his job. He was known in the agency as the Man Who Misunderstood Women. Practically all of his unattached and some of the presumably attached

115

feminine associates had gone to work on him at one time or another. But he was having none of them. Lina recalled that Beatrice had once said of him that his job was creating illusion—which ought to make him easy prey, but didn't.

Lina decided to cultivate Mr. Galleon. To be sure, his department employed experienced script writers, who were fully conversant with the advertising copy angle as well. But, she argued with herself, who in the office knew as much about Jelly Joy as she did? No one.

Galleon was not easy to see, casually. He was at the radio station during rehearsals and during the broadcasts. It was said of him that when once a week Americo's coffee program — a dramatized current events half hour — went on the air, he neither ate nor slept for twenty-four hours. *But,* thought Lina, *there must be some way.*

Her interest in radio became apparent from that day forward. Jimmy, accustomed to her turning off almost any program to which he chanced to be listening, was gratified to find her as intent as he. Sometimes too intent. She asked for tickets to the various Americo broadcasts controlled by her agency and, of course, procured them. Jimmy went with her once and returned vowing he would never go again. He wished to preserve his illusions, he told her. On three separate Sundays she dragged him through tours of the largest networks, and went to the library for books on broadcasting, studied trade magazines dealing with script writing, made herself as intelligent as possible on the subject.

In June, a year after she entered the agency, she was given a two weeks' vacation. Jimmy said, when she announced the date to him, "As you've waited so long you could have waited a little longer. . . . I don't think there's a chance — but I'll try. I hate like hell to ask favors, and you know it."

Because he didn't ask favors — when he did, his superiors listened to reason. He was given his early vacation and found that Lina had no idea of going camping with him. She consented to spend a week-end in Philadelphia with his cousins, complained of the heat and the crowded quarters of the small house, but made herself so charming that Sam Gage, slapping Jimmy on the back over a bedtime highball, informed him, "You certainly did right by yourself, Jim — she's a grand girl. I wish Mary took as much interest in my job as *she* does in yours."

They went up to Beatrice's cottage for the second week-end. But the rest of the time they stayed in town. Lina had made a new friend in the agency. This was Stella Jarvis, secretary to the president. Stella was no longer young, and certainly had never been pretty. But she was an efficient woman and practically indispensable to Mr. Harcourt.

Lina, finding that Miss Jarvis's vacation coincided with hers and that she was not leaving town because of an invalid mother, asked her twice to go with herself and Jimmy on the little trips in the car. They went for the day, with a picnic lunch. Jimmy, when urged, scrambled around among his male acquaintances and produced a fourth. Stella, hard-working and a little flattered to be singled out by Lina, whom she considered extremely clever but rather in the Beatrice Harris class, had a very good time. On the evening of the second trip as they were returning to town through the soft green twilight, she said:

"I hope you'll come up to the apartment for dinner some time. Of course, on account of Mother, we live very quietly, but I'd love to have you."

Jimmy asked later, tearing at a wilted collar:

"Now, why, Lina? Stella's all right, I like her a lot, but — this sudden enthusiasm? And she isn't one of Beatrice's gang."

"Oh," said Lina carelessly, "I get tired of that crowd sometimes. And Stella's so nice. Poor thing, she doesn't have much fun. We'll have to be very nice to her."

Dutifully she went to dinner at Stella's, listened to her interminable conversation about her sister's children, stifled her yawns, and looked warningly at Jimmy whenever he appeared watery-eyed and stifled, suppressing his own, and at parting told Stella sweetly that she'd had a marvelous time and did so hope she could come again. She sent a basket of flowers to the invisible Mrs. Jarvis and waited.

It wasn't until she had been back at work for several weeks, and until she'd been to luncheon several times with Stella, to Beatrice's open amazement, that she met Harry Galleon, as she had hoped to meet him, socially.

Mrs. Jarvis was better. Stella felt that she could give something in the nature of a small party. She asked Lina and Jimmy, another young married couple, her sister and her husband, and his brother, Harry Galleon, for two tables of bridge and a rarebit afterward. They progressed and played for prizes, which afflicted Jimmy sorely as he played a very good game, but he bore up nobly under the evening, buoyed up by a sense of amazement at Lina. Lina, who hated bridge!

Lina, playing with Harry Galleon, smiled at him over her cards. "I'd no idea," she said mendaciously, "that you and Stella were related, or, if I had, I'd forgotten. How nice to see you — I mean really see you. At the office all one catches are the most fleeting and wild-eyed glimpses."

Galleon laughed. He asked, "Am I really so wild-eyed?"

"Oh, yes," said Lina calmly, "and I don't blame you. This radio business must be — But we're holding up the game."

During supper she sat beside him on a couch and discussed broadcasting with an intelligence that astonished him. She had one or two sound criticisms to make of his programs and her praise was not too unrestrained. Galleon, who did not often indulge in bridge — and rarebit, and had come only because Stella begged him to — he was very fond of Stella — found himself having a much better time than he had anticipated. He said, "I've seen some of your campaign copy; it's very clever."

"I'm pretty new at it," Lina told him. "I wish you'd let me talk to you some time. Of course, your job is appealing to the ear and to the imagination while mine's strictly visual. Still, there's a lot I can learn from you. I've wanted to, a long time. But I didn't have the nerve. You're so awfully busy."

"Like to go to a program with me some night?" he asked her. He had known her, of course. He spoke to her in passing at the office, his brain automatically registered the fact that she was unusually pretty. But how pretty he had never realized until tonight. Of course, the dinner frock made a difference.

"I'd love to," cried Lina, her eyes shining.

It was a long time since George Onslow had mentioned that Jelly Joy might go on the air. Lina had done a lot of spadework since: the books, the broadcasting station, the trips with Stella, the careful cultivation of Stella's friendship. All worth it . . .

At home that night Jimmy said sleepily, "Don't know but what as a steady diet I prefer

Stella and her pals to Beatrice's. Nice tonight, wasn't it? That young couple — what's their name? — Martin. I liked them, didn't you? And Galleon. What on earth did you find to talk so much to Harry Galleon about? Who is he anyway?"

"Stella's sister's brother-in-law," said Lina.

"I know that. But isn't he with your outfit? You've never mentioned him before."

"He's on the radio end," said Lina. "Of course, I was interested to talk to him. There's a bare possibility that Jelly Joy may go on the air," she said carelessly. "Jimmy, help me, will you? I've caught my hair on a hook and can't get this dress off."

While he helped her untangle the bright strands with big, careful fingers, stripping the frock from her slender, fragrant person, he thought, *So that's it, is it?* He was beginning to see daylight, if very dimly.

Chapter Eight:

ANGEL ON THE MAKE

On a very warm night in July Lina went with Harry Galleon to the Americo Snowhite Flour program. Snowhite had an eight-o'clock spot and Lina met Galleon at the studio some hour before the scheduled time, and sat in the room with him and the cast of the evening's revue performance and watched while they ran through the show and were timed. The guest speaker usual on such programs was nervous and hurried over his lines, the control room swore as his voice reached them, and altogether there was the usual hysterical background preceding even so established a program as the Snowhite hour.

"But why on earth?" asked Jimmy, not too impatiently, when she told him of her plans.

"I'm interested," she answered quickly. "And if this other program goes over, perhaps I'll have a chance at it —"

"Okay," said Jimmy. "I'll hold down the fort. Run along and amuse yourself."

It being practically impossible to park near the studio, Lina did not drive her own car and refused Jimmy's offer to drive her down and wait for her. "Nonsense," she said briskly; "you'd be bored to death. You're better off at home, listening in — unless," she added, not too enthusiastically, "you want to come up with me. I'm sure Mr. Galleon wouldn't mind."

"Well, *I* would," said Jimmy. "Air conditioned or not, this is no night to spend in a broadcasting station. I'll be seeing you."

Lina taxied over and became a fascinated listener from the first to the last word and note uttered and played between the walls of Studio E. She sat during the actual broadcasting in the sponsors' small audience room and watched the studio clock's second hand as if her life depended on it. Galleon was everywhere at once, conferring with the production and program directors and the announcer. The light flashed on the announcer's panel and he touched a switch. They were on the air.

It was a network program and expensive. Lina found herself thinking, *Suppose they pull the wrong plug!*

The program was over. "Take it away," said the engineer in the control room, and another program went forth from another studio. Lina emerged breathless and excited from the little glassed-in room. Galleon met her smiling. "Like it?" he asked.

"I'm crazy about it. Golly," said Lina childishly, "I envy you your job."

"You wouldn't if you had it," he said. "Clients are bad enough. But when they become sponsors! Well that's something else again. How about a drink of something cold?"

They went downstairs to a drugstore in the building. Lina, perched on a high stool, drank lemonade and talked about the program. Long after the last sweetly acid drop had vanished from her glass she was still talking and Galleon was listening with interest and indulgence.

He taxied her home and left her at the apartment house. "It's been such fun," she said, giving him her hand. "I'm awfully grateful to you."

"No," he said, "I'm the grateful one. I was going a little stale on my job but you — you're so darned enthusiastic!" He looked at her, smiling, a personable young man with a lined forehead and heavy brows. "Let's do it again," he suggested impulsively.

Lina took herself up in the elevator. When she knocked at the door there was no response. "Jimmy," she called, and beat on the panels, swearing little-girl fashion, fiercely and harmlessly. "Drat him, he's probably selected this moment for a bath," she decided. She fished her key from her purse and opened the door. "Jimmy, I had an elegant time —" she cried, entering the living-room.

But he wasn't there. He wasn't anywhere in the apartment.

At ten-thirty Lina went to bed. At eleven she was worried. She began to think of street accidents. Twice she put her hand on the telephone to call the police, hospitals. By twelve she was frantic. Something *had* happened.

She couldn't stay in bed. She walked the floor in her flimsy nightgown and then because, despite the heat, she was chilly and her teeth chattered with nervousness, she pulled a robe about her and went on walking. When at something prior to one o'clock she heard his key in the latch and ran to meet him, her first sickening wave of relief was followed by an irrational, wholly human anger. How *dare* he be all right when she had worried herself to death!

Her voice shook, and the tears were not far away. She cried, as he walked in looking perfectly normal and not at all the worse for wear, "Where have you been? You've scared me out of my wits! What do you mean by — by —"

"Hey, not so fast," he interrupted, as her voice betrayed her and the traitor tears rolled suddenly down her cheeks. "I'm here. There's nothing the matter. I was at Beatrice's."

"Beatrice's!"

He picked her up in his arms. The tears miraculously dried, and she struggled furiously. He ordered, "Quit kicking," and strode into the bedroom with her, tossed her on the bed and his hat on the chifforobe.

Lina sat up very straight. "Jimmy Hall," she said solemnly, "I'll never forgive you the longest day I live. I've been nearly out of my mind."

Jimmy grinned. Now that she looked at him he did look rather gay. Not unpleasantly so. Just gayer than she had seen him in a long time. He

125

said gravely, "Pappy, I believe the gal loves me."

"I don't," denied Lina furiously. "Why did you go out?"

"I didn't know I had to stay at home," he replied reasonably. He sat down on the edge of the bed and locked his hands about his knees and regarded his pretty wife with pleasure.

"It's a short story," he said. "Beatrice called up about eight to say that she was having a few people in — unexpected like. Happened after she left the office — and would you and I come on over."

"But —" began Lina, and then stopped. Beatrice had known that she was going to the broadcast with Galleon, she had told her so that morning. It was not loyalty to her friend that halted her indignant tongue, but a more feminine reason. If Beatrice was beginning to connive — yes, the word was connive — to get Jimmy without his wife, far be it from Lina to flatter him by telling him so.

"Well, then," continued Jimmy, "when she found you had deserted me she said, 'Come on over alone, then; why mope all evening? It's cool on the terrace and there are mixed drinks. Very mixed.' "

"You might have left me a note," said Lina.

"On the pincushion? It hadn't come to that." He rose and began to undress. "I had a pretty good time," he said vaguely.

"Who was there?"

"Oh, her ham Hamlet and some new people. A girl called Anita something. Never did hear the last name. Nice little number."

"Pretty?"

"So-so." He turned and looked at her. "Not jealous, are you, by any chance?" he inquired thoughtfully.

"Of course not. But I'm still mad," she said vigorously. "I almost called the police."

"I thought I'd have to too," he informed her; "the Thespian boy friend started acting up. You know. Declamations."

"Well," said Lina coldly, "hurry, will you? I'm tired. And I have to work tomorrow."

"The same thought occurs to me," said Jimmy agreeably.

What bothered her most, what kept her awake long after he slept, was the conviction that she'd not seen him in as high spirits for a long time. He hadn't missed her, she thought, fear like a small cold snake coiled at her heart. He hadn't missed her at all!

She did not tell herself that she hadn't missed him either. But Galleon was business. Galleon hadn't given a party and introduced her to a dark and handsome stranger. She leaned across the small space intervening between the beds and shook Jimmy's arm.

"Where's the fire?" he demanded drowsily.

"Jimmy, was she a brunette?"

"Who?" asked Jimmy crossly.

"Anita What's-her-name."

"She," said Jimmy definitely, with the ghost of a laugh, "has green hair. Like pea soup. Also, she's cross-eyed. Go to sleep."

She slept finally, and in the morning found her anger had not evaporated. It had been a little sidetracked during her conversation with the errant Jimmy but now it returned. She viewed him coldly over the morning grapefruit.

"You probably drank too much," she stated.

"No," said Jimmy, a trifle heavy-eyed, "I didn't. I don't, in the heat. You know that."

"Cooped up in a stuffy apartment, all smoke and noise —"

"We sat on the terrace," he said. "Elegant view of the river."

"With a lot of crazy people!"

"They're your friends," Jimmy reminded her.

"I didn't say they weren't," she snapped, to the obvious interest of Kate-by-the-day.

"Look here," said Jimmy, trying to keep his temper. "I don't complain when you run around with any Tom, Dick, or Harry who happens to be able to give you a boost in your damned agency. And, by the way, that's why I had such a pleasant evening. No one mentioned agency in my presence. Half the time I wonder if you're talking percentages or cribbage scores. Anyway, I was spared that last night. And I had fun."

She said, "You usually crab about Beatrice's parties."

"This one," stated Jimmy, "was different."

During the morning she betook herself into Beatrice's office, where Beatrice, like a black-banged goddess, sat surrounded by veils of smoke.

"Come in," she invited. "Not that I'm glad to see you this morning — or anyone. The last silly wench and the last dismal male didn't leave my place till three this morning. Jimmy was one of the early homing pigeons; you have him well trained."

Lina said, "You called up and asked us both. You *knew* I wasn't home."

"Sure," admitted Beatrice, grinning like a gargoyle by Elizabeth Arden, "sure I knew it. What's it to you? I was just curious to see how Jimmy ticked when you weren't along. He did all right. I suppose you told him that I knew you were gallivanting with Galleon, the radio miracle man?"

"No," said Lina, "I didn't."

"You're smarter than I thought. Don't look as if the world were one step nearer the revolution. Do Jimmy good to go out without you now and then. I have no intentions regarding him, dishonorable or otherwise. Not now at any rate. I'm booked for, possibly, a year's run," said Beatrice carelessly. "But I'm warning you, Lina, don't be too sure of that young man. Oh, I know you celebrated your first anniversary in June — with a memorial service in the old Wop restaurant where you used to revel in hard spumoni and soft glances. But you're forgetting to

be the Little Woman. You're the Big Businesswoman instead. It may be more fun — I dare say
I've proved it — but it isn't always sensible. And
before you go off in a pet allow me to inform you
that there is now a blonde who shall be nameless
who thinks your Jimmy is the Prince of Wales,
Cary Grant and Noel Coward."

"It must be Elsa Maxwell," said Lina
acidulously.

Beatrice laughed. "You're coming on," she
commented appreciatively.

"I know," said Lina; "her name's Anita."

"So he told you? Silly of him," said Beatrice,
yawning. "Well, *verbum sap*. And you know
what happens to saps. Run along and peddle
your tabloids because if I'm not busy God
knows I ought to be."

At the door Lina turned.

"I'm not afraid of competition," she said. "I'd
like to meet Anita."

Anita was a visiting fireman. She was a little
thing from Georgia. The accents of the sunny
South pervaded her trivial conversation. She
was untidy, terribly pretty, and as clinging as
Lastex. She was just a Home Girl and she was
having a quite too marvelous time in New York
through the kind offices of an aunt who had,
unfortunately for Beatrice, gone to school with
Beatrice's mother.

Lina, encountering Anita, was unperturbed.
What Jimmy — or anyone — could see in that
brainless little bit of beaten biscuit! Yet she

wasn't so brainless, Lina discovered, too quickly for her own comfort. And she was certainly Georgia's shining example of a special Southern brand of Canadian Royal Mounted.

Lina and Jimmy went to Beatrice's cottage for a week-end. Anita was there. She said to Lina, on the first day, "I wonder if you know how lucky you are. When I found out Jimmy was married I'd like to have died. He's the *sweetest* thing!"

Jimmy, within earshot, would like to have died too, looking uncomfortable but, Lina remarked, complacent as well. She thought, *Men are such fools,* and later made the mistake of telling him so.

"Well, if you like professional Southerners —"

"I'd hardly call her that."

" 'Dixie' on her handkerchief!" said Lina in disgust, in the seclusion of the guestroom they occupied. "Round blue eyes, natural curly hair, gardenia perfume, and runs in her stockings!"

"She hasn't much money," said Jimmy. "Her people are hard up."

"I suppose they lost all they had in the Civil War," said Lina.

"Well, yes," Jimmy admitted, feeling idiotic. But damn it, Anita had told him so. "What's it to you?"

"Nothing. If she's so poor, why doesn't she get out and work?" asked Lina. "Provided there is anything she can do, which I doubt."

"It's queer," said Jimmy, "but she doesn't

131

seem to mind being poor. And she likes to stay home."

"Why doesn't she then?" inquired Lina.

"Oh, for heaven's sake!" Jimmy flung himself away from the window and a contemplation of Beatrice's tended lawn. "I didn't come up here to quarrel with you. I'm going out, I've a croquet date."

"All the best people play croquet now," murmured Lina. "I'll bet Dixie — Anita to you — is a champion!"

By September Anita had gone. She went reluctantly because she simply adored New York, "You all don't know how lucky you are!" but at the same time she would be glad to see Peachtree Street again and there was a certain young man — "Of course, I'm going to marry him. We'll be poor as churchmice — but we won't care. He just made me come North. He said, 'Here's your chance to meet a millionaire, Dixie.' But I wouldn't change my Pete for all the millionaires in the world."

"Especially as you didn't meet any," murmured Beatrice, to whom these last remarks were addressed, in accents impossible to reproduce in print.

When she had gone, Lina faced Beatrice triumphantly. "She wasn't much of a menace after all," she said. "Jimmy hasn't given her a thought."

"He hasn't given her more than a thought, you mean," said Beatrice. "I didn't think she was a menace, in person. But," more gravely than was her custom, "these home gals have something on the eight ball. They're not so dumb. And the fact that Anita thought Jimmy was too too clever and too too marvelous, or, at all events, told him so, was a change from his accustomed fare."

"What do you mean?" asked Lina sharply.

"I mean," said Beatrice, "that your Jimmy is a man, like other men. Oh, head and shoulders above, I grant you," she added, laughing, "but it's as well to remind him of the fact. After all, he must get tired hearing you tell him how wonderful *you* are!"

"If that's what you think I —" began Lina.

"That's what I know you do," said Beatrice. "You see, I do it myself, I'll never learn. My error. And yours. But you may be able to re-form. I can't, somehow. Hardened sinner, that's me."

In September something happened which drove all thoughts of Anita out of Lina's head. Americo had definitely decided to put Jelly Joy on the air, featuring the new package as well as the regular sizes. And Harry Galleon took Lina out to lunch and suggested that she go into conference on the program. They had decided on a well-known orchestra, a male singer with a national reputation, and a short sketch depicting the trials and tribulations of a young couple, newly married. The agency employed continuity writers, with experience and in some cases even creative talent. But Lina could write the announcements and with her special knowledge of the product make herself generally useful.

In the first week of October the program had its *première*. The sponsors were there in force: two of Americo's heads, the sales manager in charge of Jelly Joy, and the manager of the plant where the product was manufactured. Mr. Shaw represented the advertising agency, and there were assorted wives of assorted shapes and coloring. Galleon, of course, was in the studio, and so was Lina.

The clock warned, the light flashed, the switch was thrown, and the home life of Mr. and Mrs. Smith, preceded by music, was on the air.

After it was over there was nothing to do but listen to the mingled criticism and congratulations, fears and hopes of the sponsors and wait for the fan mail, if any.

"Mr. and Mrs. Smith" caught on. The public loved them; it ate them up, with the result that it would soon begin to eat Jelly Joy at a rate hitherto unprecedented in its brief annals. Advertising copy released through magazines and other media carried notices to the effect that the Smiths would be on the air every Wednesday night at 8:30; those who sent in two package covers would receive photographs of the members of the cast. An enterprising women's store designed a "Mrs. Smith" frock, and the retail grocers living in or near New York, or planning vacations there, bombarded Americo for tickets to the broadcasts for themselves, their wives, their children, and their relatives.

Lina, poring over the notebooks which Jimmy kept for her, reread several episodes, conversations he had overheard between grocers and housewives and, marveling at the ability of the American woman for taking the world into her confidence, rewrote them and showed them to Galleon.

"I thought," she said hesitantly, "that for the fifteen-minute break something like this might vary the commercial announcements. We have three. If one in the middle were different — Other programs do it. A few seconds' sketch — dialogue, say, built around a conversation between a woman and a grocer. The trouble is," she added, "that in the announcements of this type the woman never seems quite real."

Galleon said, as she had hoped, "Why don't you do it?"

By November Lina was on the air. The continuity writer devised brief, amusing dialogue and a male member of the Smith cast doubled for the grocer. Lina had a voice to which the microphone was kind. The addition to the program was received with enthusiasm. Mr. Shaw, calling her into his office for congratulations after the first evening, made it perfectly plain that the agency was proud of her.

She still saw a good deal of Harry Galleon. She believed him to be a little in love with her. It suited her to keep him that way but she had no intention of permitting him to become an embarrassment. Beatrice, walking along the corridors with her one frosty morning, looked at her and laughed. She said pleasantly:

"Sometimes, Lina, with those big gray eyes and that mop of fair hair you look like a Christmas tree angel — but an angel on the make!"

Chapter Nine:

A PROMISE COMES HOME TO ROOST

On their second Christmas together, Lina, mindful of Jimmy's curious sentiment, stayed at home. She asked people to drop in during the evening for a buffet supper, and Jimmy found himself serving in the triple capacity of host, bartender, and waiter until early the next morning. Beatrice came, with a troupe of her "unattached" friends, Tad and Nancy looked in for a moment on their way back from Tad's people in Jersey, Harry Galleon came for an hour or two, George Onslow for somewhat longer, and even Stella, after her mother had gone to sleep, taxied down for a little while. "You would think," commented Jimmy, viewing the remains after they had gone, "that they had no homes."

Glass-rings on the tables, heaped cigarette butts in the ash trays, a hole burned through the upholstered arm of a chair, plates parked in the most unlikely places, half a sandwich ground into the carpet by a careless foot . . . stuffiness and smoke.

"Kate," said Lina wearily, "makes me tired. She could have come as well as not. I counted on her, or I would have had the caterer's man."

"You knew she asked for the day off."

"Of course. But I never dreamed, when I decided to have the party, that she wouldn't return in the evening to help. I offered her good pay."

"Funny, isn't it," said Jimmy, "you can't buy everything?"

"Must you talk in clichés?"

"Well, well, I forgot to take them off," said Jimmy gravely.

Lina didn't answer. She said, yawning her way into the bedroom, "Oh, leave the mess. She can clear it up in the morning. Tomorrow's Tuesday, worse luck, and we have to work."

Jimmy opened some windows, and dumped the contents of ash trays in a big Benares brass bowl. He said, after a moment, "Kate has the right idea. She has a couple of half-grown kids. Why shouldn't she spend the day with them, where she belongs?"

Lina, running water in the bathroom, didn't hear.

January. . . . Lina worked hard at the office, and suffered recurrent agonies in which she felt that she hadn't another shot in the locker, that she was written out, that she had gone completely stale. But she had found a remedy for these terrifying lapses: there was always George Onslow, or Harry Galleon, or Mr. Shaw, or Beatrice, or even Jimmy when she could take time to be alone with him. They were bound to have fresh ideas, present new angles, if she could draw them out cleverly, without obvious-

138

ness. She needed only the ghost of an idea, a lead, a hint upon which she could seize and elaborate.

There were times when Jimmy Hall believed he had married a cross between an adding machine and a typewriter. Yet he often reproached himself for his discontent. Lina could be sweeter than most women. Now and then they had an evening or a holiday alone, during which she seemed to forget weariness, the agency, and those things which were so important to her. Then she was yielding and provocative by turns, informed with a faint, captivating mischief, and seemingly wholly his own.

In common with the majority of men, Jimmy longed for the complete possession of the woman he loved and had married. He was intelligent and he had, since his marriage, grown up to an alarming degree. He was alone a good deal, because of Lina's weekly evenings at the studios and her occasional overtime at the office. He read, he went out with men of his acquaintance, many of them unknown to his wife. He was growing slowly into the knowledge that it is humanly impossible to enter into a complete possession of another person, mind and spirit. But surely the modern woman, with her restlessness, her greed for individuality, her insistence upon a career, denied more of herself than had her predecessors?

Poor kid, he thought, *it isn't her fault. She was pitchforked into this. And she's always been ambi-*

tious, a fighter. It isn't her fault either if she's blind on one side and can't see all she's missing.

She took on the coloring of others like a chameleon. Whether consciously or not, Jimmy wasn't sure. He watched her with Beatrice and saw how brittle she became, hard, with a shining veneer, as styled and durable, as metallic and comfortless as the new furniture. He watched her with Stella, with whom she was softer, charming, even deferential. He saw her at rare intervals with Harry Galleon, wholly feminine, almost hesitant in voicing her opinions, always waiting for Galleon's guidance. And he occasionally managed to look at her detachedly, in relation to herself. She could be as sharp as acid, or as sweet as syrup. Sometimes she was like a tired child, wanting spoiling, consolation. Sometimes she was an adult woman, arguing with him in the easy patter of the day, talking psychology, voicing frank and recently read views which shocked him slightly, and set him wondering whether these scientific and medical discoveries relative to the working of the human mind and physiology had really advanced the world as far as the discoverers claimed. And there were other times when she was, as nearly as possible, a businessman.

What he was learning, without putting terms to it, was that Lina was a personality of many personalities. Each had its separate compartment, and functioned to complete her as a whole person. In one such compartment was her love for Jimmy Hall. It was narrow and it was deep and it did not invade, nor pervade, the other compartments. It belonged to her and to him and had nothing to do with the rest of her life. If sometimes he told himself, in a dark dismay of spirit, that she did not love him as much as he loved her, it was merely the world-old cry of the genuine lover who for his much-loving expects more than a little. That which no lover regards or understands is capacity. The pitcher, going to the well, returns full and brimming over, and the cup returns as full as the measure of its capacity will permit.

Coming out of the broadcasting station one night with Galleon, Lina bumped squarely into Bill Ryder. She had not seen him since her marriage. Now he advanced upon her, suffered the introduction to Galleon with bare courtesy, and announced that now he had found her he was not going to lose her again. He had his car around the corner, he would drive her home. "We're old friends," he explained to Galleon. "I've been carrying the torch for — how long is it, Lina? — over a year and a half."

He was so insistent that, short of a scene, she could not deny him. He drove her, by the longest possible route, to the apartment. He asked her a thousand questions and did not wait for answers. He knew all about her, he declared, how far she'd gone, where she was going. "And you would get married," he declared sorrowfully, "would hamper your stride with the w.k. manacles. Lina, you're nerts."

"I don't think so," she told him with spirit. "Jimmy and I are very happy."

"When am I going to see you again?"

"You might," she suggested, "come up to the apartment some night."

"And view young married love in its most sickening form: domesticity, slippers, radio, evening papers? I'm not in my dotage. Look. I'll ankle down to your office some day and take you to lunch."

"I doubt it," said Lina serenely. But she felt amused and stimulated. She could handle Bill Ryder; she had proved that. And he was entertaining. No woman likes to feel that she is discounted stock after marriage. Her relations with Harry Galleon were different. She was shrewd enough to realize that Galleon was a sober man, a person of integrity. So long as he was convinced that she was happily married, she would have no trouble with him. He would help her as much as lay in his power, and there would be no strings attached. But once she even suggested that she was not emotionally satisfied in her marriage, even for the sake of a mild flirtation, she would have trouble with him. Galleon took women seriously, and Bill Ryder did not.

He helped her out of the car and they stood talking at the door, where Jimmy found them when he came back from mailing a letter. The trivial thought flashed through Lina's mind as he came up that she'd always said there should be a mail chute in the apartment.

"Hi, Jimmy," said Ryder easily, "how's the boy? Bumped into Lina at Radio Center and thought I'd see she got home safely."

They shook hands, exchanged a word or two and then Ryder turned away. " 'By," he said, "be seeing you." He drove off and Jimmy and Lina went on upstairs.

"Well," inquired Jimmy when the door closed behind them, "and how did that happen?"

"He was outside, when Harry Galleon and I left the building," replied Lina, taking off her things. She went to her bedroom to hang up her new fur coat, and Jimmy followed her.

"Fortuitous, wasn't it?"

"No," said Lina. "If you don't believe me, that's your hard luck."

"How long have you been seeing Ryder?"

"Don't be silly," said Lina crossly. "I haven't laid eyes on him since we were married, and you can't take that tone with me, Jimmy. If you don't trust me, that's just too bad. If I want to see Bill Ryder, I'll see him. There's no reason why I shouldn't —"

"When did you stop loving me?" he asked dully. It was absurd, but he had to say it.

Lina stamped her foot. "You complete idiot —" she began and then she looked at him. He was sitting on the edge of the bed, slumped forward, and something in the haggard, tired lines

143

of his face touched and frightened her. She forgot what she was going to say; she forgot her anger, which was not unmixed with guilt — oh, not that she'd done anything! She ran forward and flung herself into his arms.

"I've never stopped," she cried, "I never shall. Oh, Jimmy, don't be so foolish. You know I love you, you *must* know it. There's no one else, there never will be."

He believed her. And the curious thing was that he was right.

Nevertheless, she went to lunch with Ryder the second time he asked her. The first time she refused and Beatrice, strolling into her office, heard her. Beatrice, when Ryder had been presented, said casually, "Too bad you're at a loose end for lunch, Mr. Ryder. As it happens, so am I."

They went away together, laughing. Lina looked after them. She and Beatrice had had a date. She went off to hunt up Stella and the next time Ryder stopped in, she said indifferently, "Oh, very well," and that was that. She did it only, she assured herself, to get even with Beatrice. Beatrice had taking ways.

She had telling ways also. She told Jimmy all about it the next time they were together. "You should have seen Lina's face," she informed him; "it was priceless. So might the dog in the manger have looked, provided he was very blond and pretty. And I walked off with the boy friend. The next time she didn't turn him down."

"Why did you do it?" he asked Lina when they were alone.

She had an intuition that now if ever honesty would be the best policy.

"I had no intention of going out to lunch with him," she declared, "but Beatrice made me so darned mad. So — the next time — Please don't mind, Jimmy; it wasn't much fun, really. Except hearing about Americo, from the office end. That was fun. I don't get much news, except what you tell me."

Jimmy was silent a moment. He had come to a conclusion. He had been coming to it ever since the morning after their quarrel. One sees things in a different light the morning after.

He said, "When we were married there was some talk of a partnership. When one of the partners decides to go his own way, then I think the other one is justified —"

"What do you mean?" she asked quickly.

"Go out with Ryder," he said, trying to forget how much it cost him to say it, "or with anyone else. You asked me if I trusted you. I do. Then you must trust me too."

"Who is she?" asked Lina, too quietly.

Jimmy laughed. "Does it matter? Frankly, Lina, I haven't seen anyone with whom I'd care to spend the evening — or the lunch hour. But —"

For some time now it had become an established custom that on Wednesday nights when Lina was at the studio Jimmy went out "stag."

Occasionally she phoned that she'd stay and work in the office, get something to eat and go on to the studio afterward. Kate had Wednesdays off and Jimmy would go out or get himself something to eat. It now occurred to her that perhaps Wednesdays were not always stag. When she asked him, he said, "Why, no. Now and then one of the men drags a girl or two along. Last week, for instance. We went to the movies."

Toward the middle of February Lina came home late, and tired, to find Jimmy waiting. When she opened the door her first impression was that he had been drinking. He was flushed, his eyes unusually bright, his red hair looked disheveled, as if he had been running his hands through it. But when he seized her and kissed her, she knew his excitement was not artificially stimulated.

"Jimmy, what's happened?"

"Beginning next month I'm district manager for Westchester. They've moved Watkins up a step. I'm to have a free hand and a little better than five thousand dollars," he told her.

"Jimmy!"

Her instant reaction was of happiness for him. He'd worked hard, he deserved it, it was what he wanted. She had forgotten what that district managership entailed for her. In the next breath he reminded her of it.

"As soon as you've caught your breath, Mrs. Hall," he said, "you can sit right down and write your resignation, effective March first."

146

Chapter Ten:

A BITTER DECISION

Jimmy's voice was confident, more so than he felt. His excited enthusiasm and triumph were tinctured with trepidation. But he persisted in the assumption that Lina had made a bargain with him and that she would hold to it. There was, after he had spoken, an unnatural quiet in the room, and during its brief tenure he watched the blood drain from her face. The slight amount of rouge she affected was startling against the pallor.

She said evenly, "You can't possibly mean that, Jimmy!"

"Of course," he reassured her, "I mean it. Stop standing there staring at me as if I were a ghost. You — you look like one yourself. Perhaps I shouldn't have sprung it on you like that. But — God, Lina, if you knew what this means to me!"

She shrugged herself out of her coat, let it fall to the floor; put up her hand, pulled off her hat and dropped it and her handbag on a table. She did not sit down. She put her fingers on the polished surface of the table, behind her, and steadied herself. She asked him, after a moment, "I do know what it means to you; but — can't you realize what *my* work means to me?"

He had expected protest, and had braced

147

himself for it, but he was not prepared for an almost savage hostility, the more frightening because it was so deathly cold and measured.

"Sure," he said, "sure I do. But you promised, Lina. It — it was because of that promise that I persuaded myself that our marriage would become something real and honest, something more important to us both than anything else."

She said, "It can't be very important to you if you feel your pride matters more than my happiness!"

"My pride!" he repeated, staring at her.

"Exactly. What else is it? You can't stand the thought of *your* wife — your goods and chattel — working. You can't stand it because I've made more money than you, because my every thought isn't for your comfort. If you could stand it, if your absurd pride didn't block every common-sense thought you ever had, you'd realize that there's no reason why I shouldn't go on with my job. What if you are going to have five thousand a year? We can live better on ten thousand, can't we?"

She crossed the room and sat down, lighting a cigarette with unsteady fingers. Kate came in from the kitchen to announce dinner; Lina waved her away with an imperious petulance. Kate retired to her kitchen, shook her head, and concentrated on keeping things hot.

Jimmy, standing over Lina, looked down on her. His hands itched to seize her, to shake her into sanity, to smack her into docility. He thrust them into his pockets and said, "So you feel that way. All right, it's my pride then, I don't care what you call it. I'm a fool possibly, even probably. I just happen to feel this way, that's all. I want you — for myself. I want my wife. I don't want a woman who spends nine-tenths of her time wondering how far and how fast she can climb in business. I asked you to make me a certain promise. You made it, and you'll keep it, or else —"

"Or else what?" asked Lina sharply.

"Or else we'll come to some other arrangement," he replied wearily. "You haven't very long to make up your mind. I intend to sublet this place if I can. Our lease runs till June. We're going to move into my district and that's final. Either you go with me . . . or, so far as I am concerned, you can stay here alone."

She said again, her lips stiff, "You don't mean that, Jimmy."

"I do. You've been getting away with murder. Well, you won't any more. You'll play ball. I was crazy when I thought you meant to keep that promise when you made it. Perhaps men have different standards from women. I dunno. Anything to keep me quiet, I suppose. Well, you made it and you'll keep it or else you can break it and the hell with it. I'll get along."

He looked at her and hated her; he looked at her and loved her so much that it was sheer agony; he loved her small, white face with its look of defiance and anger; he loved the fair hair curling back from her brow in disorder and the great gray eyes, hard now and shining, the pupils black and dilated. He wanted to kiss her and beat her. And more than anything he wanted to conquer her — if not through love for him, then in any way, force or threats, it didn't matter. It was definitely vital that for once the victory should lie to him.

"You're unutterably selfish," she said slowly. "You want me to give up something I've worked for, something which means so much to me. You want me to bury myself with you out in the country, and do housework to pass the time away. You want me to live on five thousand dollars a year —"

"Yes," he broke in, "I do. Five thousand dollars a year. A mere pittance. Suppose you take a look along the bread lines some cold evening and ask the men standing there what five thousand dollars a year would mean to them. Suppose you ask some of the women who wait for those men and wonder how they're going to feed their kids. You make me sick. You've delusions of grandeur. Five thousand a year isn't enough for you. Ten thousand isn't either. You want — God knows what you want, but it's perfectly clear that you don't want *me*."

Her face quivered and broke. She said, her voice shaking, "Jimmy — I've never seen you — you never talked to me like this — I — Oh, why," she wailed, "why can't you be reasonable? We'd have such a lovely life —"

"Lovely," he agreed, "perfectly divine." His silly words bit like acid. "I'd be crazy about it. I wonder how often I'd see you. You'd find commuting pretty damned difficult — with so much necessary overtime at the office to say nothing of your magnificent radio work!"

Lina jumped to her feet. If she was white before, now she was scarlet. She cried, her voice rising, "If you're insinuating —"

"I'm not insinuating anything. I'm telling you. I'm past anything else. Look here, Lina, you're a clever girl. But you're not as clever as you think you are. You believe you're getting places on your own. Well, you're not. You're getting places because you've pumped me dry of every bit of information I can give you, because you're leading Galleon around by a ring through his nose, because you're willing to have lunch now and then with Onslow and to flatter him until he tells you just what you want to know. You use everybody. Don't think I don't know it. It took me a long time but I'm not quite as dumb as you imagine."

"You needn't say any more," she told him. "Or perhaps you'd better say it plainer. So I'm not good in my job, am I? It takes you great big strong brilliant men to help me every step of the way? I don't get there by brains, do I, I get there through sex appeal?"

"You've put it very well," he told her. "An expert diagnosis."

The room was shrill and ugly with their clamor. The tension was almost tangible. Kate looked out from the kitchen and retreated again. The chops would burn and the soup suffered with standing. She thought philosophically, *Well, if they bust up, I'll be looking for another job.* Her sympathies were all with Jimmy. She disliked Lina. Not that Lina wasn't always pleasant to her, if a little crotchety at times. But Kate, being Kate, had no use for these hard young ones who didn't know when they were well off.

Lina sat down again. She began to cry, from nerves, from anger, and perhaps from strategy. Jimmy plunged his hands deeper in his pockets. He moved closer to her without touching her. He said quietly:

"I'm sorry, Lina, that it had to be like this. But — either you love me enough to come my way or you don't. And if you don't — well, that's that — we'll call the whole thing off. It's up to you."

"It's not *fair*," she protested, sobbing, "not fair to put it like that. It's taking such an advantage. You *know* I love you."

"But not enough," he said.

He went out into the little hall and she called after him, controlling her voice, "Where are you going?"

"Just out," he answered. "There's no use staying. We aren't getting anywhere. Perhaps you'll think it over and come to some conclusion."

The door slammed. Lina jumped up again and whirled herself into the kitchen, looking like a miniature blond Fury. She said to Kate, "Never mind dinner. I'll get something later. Stop staring at me — and go on home."

Another door slammed. This time the bedroom door. Kate regarded the burnt offerings. It was a shame to waste the chops. A body couldn't bear to waste anything nowadays with people starving. She popped the chops into a paper bag and set to clearing away briskly. She'd go home, all right, but not without her dinner, which was her prerogative. She'd have it with her kids, and welcome. And meantime there was something to be salvaged here.

Lina prone on her bed heard Kate leave a little later. She was alone in the apartment. Her head ached. She felt ill. The thought of food turned her over. Jimmy was probably in a restaurant this moment attacking a large steak. Men were like that. Insensitive brutes.

She got up and washed her face and carried a wet cloth back to the bedroom with her. She kicked off her shoes and curled up her toes in their silken sheaths.

He didn't mean it.

But she was afraid that he did.

She began to visualize a suburban existence. Housework. Naturally Jimmy would expect her to do the housework and, to be honest with herself, there was no reason why she shouldn't. Just the two of them and all day on her hands!

A cleaning woman, of course, and perhaps someone by the hour to help if they entertained. But whom would they entertain? She couldn't expect her friends to trek out to heaven knew where.

She began to think of the things they'd say at the office, more particularly of what Beatrice would say, and her face burned. She wouldn't be blackmailed into this position. She'd hold out as long as he — longer, if she knew men. He'd come back again, groveling.

She put her hand on the telephone. Why not call Beatrice and make a gag of it? *What do you think's happened, darling? Jimmy's gone mid-Victorian on me — insists I give up my job because he's had a promotion. Tie that, if you can.*

No. She was afraid of what Beatrice might reply. She wasn't sure of Beatrice. She liked her better than any woman she had ever known; she'd never really been fond of a woman before. She told herself that Beatrice was her closest friend. But somehow the impulse to confide in her died a-borning.

If only there were somebody. But there wasn't. She knew what Nancy'd say. And she didn't know Stella well enough. What she wanted, of course, was not advice, but agreement and approbation.

Just because she'd promised!

Men evidently took promises seriously, when it suited them. They could break their own quickly enough and find plenty of alibis. You'd have thought she'd sworn on a stack of Bibles! Couldn't he see that things were different? When she'd made that promise she hadn't been where she was now, hadn't had as secure or as bright a future. And, of course, when he'd reminded her of it more recently she'd reassured him, any woman would; it had meant nothing, and he ought to have more sense.

Men were so sentimental.

At midnight he had not returned, and she was hungry. Her wave of physical discomfort had passed and, while her head still ached furiously, she was aware of a vast emptiness. She put on her slippers, went into the kitchen, and regarded the contents of the icebox. What had happened to those chops? Kate, of course. No servant was to be trusted. There was a chicken leg from last night and the remains of a vegetable salad. She carried them over to the breakfast nook and ate them from their containers, not bothering to find a plate. She rinsed them and her fork, set them in the sink, and found herself half a glass of milk.

She was worn out with thinking in circles and with crying. She was by turns furiously angry with Jimmy and dreadfully sorry for herself. It would come out all right, she was sure of it, but meantime she'd suffered and some day she'd repay him for that.

At one she took off her clothes and went to bed. She was still awake at three. He hadn't come in. Where was he? He might have gone to his old apartment, the one he and Kit had shared with the utility men. He still saw them occasionally. She could call there. She had no compunction about waking anyone, but if he weren't there she'd feel like a fool and the men would talk and laugh and speculate among themselves. "So Jimmy Hall's taken to staying out all night, has he, and the little woman doesn't like it?"

She'd never call before she'd put herself in such a position.

He had to come home some time, for the practical things: a shave, a clean shirt. It then occurred to her that there are barber shops and that you can buy shirts.

Kate arrived to cook breakfast and Lina spoke to her about the chops. She considered Kate's reply insolent but did nothing further about it. She hadn't the energy. She felt like something no self-respecting cat would have considered dragging in — she felt like the end of the world. And when Kate asked her, "Isn't Mr. Hall coming to breakfast?" she replied, looking at his empty place with alien eyes and drinking her own scalding coffee, "No, he isn't. He was called away last night."

She knew that the woman didn't believe her, and for once she didn't care.

When she left, a little late, for the office, Jimmy had not come home.

The day went badly. She couldn't concentrate on her work. She ripped sheet after sheet out of her typewriter, crumpled it, and tossed it in the scrap basket. Something went wrong at the engraver's and there was unutterable confusion. She wanted to ask Mr. Shaw's advice on some copy — she had found it politic to do so, now and then — but he had taken this day to remain away from the office with a cold. Beatrice strolled in and out with extreme nonchalance, and commented cruelly on her appearance. "You look like creamed salt mackerel," she remarked. And somehow the last straw was Beatrice's new frock, dark red wool with a silver belt, severe and wickedly becoming and looking as if it had cost a fortune, as it probably had.

Jimmy would expect her to dress on what he'd give her, she thought, slamming paper into the machine. Nothing of her own. Just what he'd dole out from day to day. That would be fine, wouldn't it?

Galleon poked his head in the office a little before noon and asked her if she'd care to lunch. She nodded and went on trying to work. Had Jimmy come home yet? She might ring up Kate and ask. She'd be damned if she'd give the woman the satisfaction. She didn't care if he never came home!

But she did care. That was the difficulty. If only she didn't love him. If only — Why did she have to love him? Love had nothing to do with her as a person. It was a stumbling block, a weakness, a madness.

She was so distracted at lunch, and looked so badly despite her careful titivation, that Galleon became concerned. He asked, leaning across the table in the small, quiet restaurant, "Lina, is there anything the matter? If there's anything I can do — You know I'm your friend."

It didn't make sense, she should have known better, but she had to tell someone, had to be petted and consoled and told she was ill-treated, and that it would surely come out all right, her way. She replied, her lips shaking, "It's Jimmy. We've quarreled."

"I'm sorry to hear that," he said gravely.

"He's had a promotion. He wants me to give up my job."

"Are you going to?" asked Galleon.

"I don't know." She stared at him, the gray eyes misty. "I don't see why I should. It's so unfair. I've worked so hard and I'm crazy about it."

"Surely then," said Galleon gently, "he'll understand. I suppose, being a man, I comprehend somewhat how he feels. I know that if I were in his shoes —" He broke off and smiled at her. "He'll understand," he repeated.

"No," denied Lina, "he won't. He's so — selfish. You see — before we were married, I promised him that if he ever got a district managership I would quit work —"

It was the wrong thing to say and she realized it as soon as it was said. She should never had told Galleon of that promise. Men were so idiotic about promises they hadn't made themselves. And men stuck together.

"Then," said Galleon, "I don't believe you have any choice. If you love him. You do love him, don't you, Lina?"

She would have given ten years of her life to be able to answer *no* — honestly or dishonestly. It didn't matter. But she couldn't. She said, dismayed, "Yes, I do —"

Galleon leaned back. There were heavy lines about his mouth which she had not noticed before.

"Lina, there's no use my trying to kid myself that my interest in you is purely — business and friendship. It isn't. You're a clever woman and you must have known. You've been very sweet to me, but you've made me understand that there are certain barriers. If you could tell me, and mean it, that you do not love your husband — well — But you can't. You do love him. And he's a lucky man, to have you love him enough to make this sacrifice. You will make it, of course. You're too honest and fine a person to break a promise. Whether he's right or wrong is beside the point. And perhaps you'll be happier with a home, leisure, children."

She thought, *Men are so sentimental. Jimmy talking about starving babies and now Harry Galleon with his own idea of what constitutes a happy woman.* But the thought passed quickly. She was beginning to see herself in a new and rather charming light. Big Businesswoman Gives Up Brilliant Career for Love, Home, and Husband.

A little color touched her cheeks. She said, slowly, "Perhaps you're right. I don't know."

"Make up with him," he urged her; "talk it out. You'll see. You see, you've no alternative really. You gave your word and you'll keep it. But you'll think about it first and realize perhaps that for all you are giving up you'll be repaid, a thousandfold."

Later, when they had returned to the office, she said quickly, "I haven't told anyone but you, Harry. You won't say anything yet, will you?"

"No," he pledged, "I won't. And thank you for telling me." He held her hand a moment, closely. "I'm grateful for your confidence, Lina."

Beatrice came along and grinned at them impartially. Lina withdrew her hand, murmured something, and fled to her desk. Beatrice, looking in a moment later, said, "Don't carry your impulses too far. Galleon doesn't know what it's all about. Talk about taking lollipops from infants!"

Lina snapped at her. Beatrice raised her eyebrows and withdrew. "Sorry," she murmured, "didn't realize the corns hurt today."

Toward the middle of the afternoon Onslow barged in. He smote Lina on the back and announced that he had been transferred to the

Los Angeles office — for six months or a year. "Hollywood, here I come," he said triumphantly; "week-ends in patios, cocktails served in swimming pools, an afternoon at polo or the races and all the beautiful stars just waiting open-armed for me. Boy, is this a break or is this a break? Palm Springs and Caliente, watch my smoke! Will you miss me, Lina?"

She managed to tell him that she would and that she was glad for him. When he'd gone to special the news abroad she stared blankly at her typewriter. She depended on Onslow. He was very useful to her. Without him things would not go so easily. It would be harder sledding. He was a very clever young man and an ace among copy writers. He had an unerring feeling for the weakness in her copy. Of course, Howard, the copy chief, remained and it was his job to see that every piece of work that went out of his department was as good as labor and brains and conferences could make it. But Onslow was something else again. He had a flair, an understanding of the way her mind worked, and he was as full of ideas as a porcupine is of quills.

Galleon, astonishingly, on Jimmy's side, and Onslow leaving! She felt chilly with nerves, with misgivings. She thought, *If I do stay on, no matter what Jimmy says?*

She began to think that perhaps Galleon wasn't really enough in love with her to approve such a decision. It might not be easy to win him over, to convince him of her unhappiness. And besides, she didn't love Galleon. She loved Jimmy.

She remembered something he'd said to her, before last night. About going his own way, Jimmy was attractive to women. Even to women like Beatrice, who knew dozens of men, all kinds of men. Lina hadn't for a moment believed that he meant it when he said he would leave her if she kept on with the job. He wouldn't. But if he went his way . . . ?

She discovered that her headache had returned. She went out and knocked at Howard's door and told him about it. "Splitting," she mourned. "If it's all right, I think I'll go home."

She went and Kate informed her with marked pleasure that Mr. Hall hadn't been in and that the grocery order hadn't come. Lina said shortly, "It doesn't matter. We'll eat out tonight, Kate. You can have the rest of the day off."

Then she sat down to wait.

He came in at his accustomed time. He had the slightly guilty look of a man who has put his foot down and intends to keep it there but finds the stance a little slippery. He said, "Lina, I'm sorry I went off like that."

The moment she set eyes on him she knew it was no use. They'd have to try it — his way. And besides, the office hadn't quite the pristine attraction it had had a few hours earlier. She said, smiling, "Jimmy, let's eat at Antonio's tonight . . . a sort of celebration. I'll send in my resignation tomorrow."

He made an inarticulate sound, took her in his arms and kissed her and held her as if he would never let her go. This was his hour, his moment of victory. She let him have it. And when he said, "If you knew what this means to me, Lina — Don't think I don't know really the sacrifice you're making — I do — but it means that you love me more than anything in the world —"

"And that's what counts," she replied, drawing back to look at him reprovingly. "But you were so silly to have doubted it, Jimmy. I — let's forget last night, shall we?"

He promised. It was a promise he might have found easy to keep had Lina not reminded him of it rather often in the days to follow.

Chapter Eleven:

THE PALL OF SUBURBIA

Lina's resignation from the agency caused something of a stir, but did not prove the catastrophe she had permitted herself to believe. Howard knew there were other girls who could write copy, and Mr. Shaw knew it. And as for her special knowledge of Jelly Joy, it was all down on paper and anyone who had eyes to read and a brain to retain could absorb it. It was a considerable blow to her to find herself not indispensable, but she tried to close her eyes to it, and her report to Jimmy upon what this one and what that one had said was slightly, and dramatically, colored. He felt like a brute listening, but a happy brute, a conqueror.

Beatrice was amused. "So you've gone the way of all female flesh? Well, more power to you. I think you've the right idea. I congratulate Jimmy. And I congratulate you on having a man with more will power than most. This double-income business is raising hell with our bright young men. Most of them wouldn't marry a woman who didn't contribute to the family exchequer. They've been forced into this position by us brainy gals and they're making the most of it. They have their comeuppance too, although most of us don't realize it. Good luck, sugar."

Lina's heart sank. She thought, *She's glad I'm going. Is it because she's on Jimmy's side or because she's afraid of me — afraid that I'm runner-up?*

She preferred the latter version and repeated it to Jimmy. "I believe," she said, laughing, "that Beatrice was scared of me — in the office I mean — as if I could threaten her position!"

"Of course, she was," agreed Jimmy fondly. He could afford to be a little fatuous now, afford to preserve her illusions. Moreover, he almost believed in them himself. He had been perfectly sincere in saying that she had won her way up by employing useful people. But that opinion in no way conflicted with the idea that Beatrice Harris, who had probably reached her present vantage point by the same method, could be afraid of the younger girl.

A young couple whom they knew slightly took the apartment off their hands and before that was accomplished Lina spent some time in Mount Vernon looking for a place to live. She found an apartment finally, modern and pleasant and with a view of trees and green lawns. This they took, and vacating the New York place by the first of the month, lived at a small hotel until they were settled, the apartment newly decorated, and the furniture placed.

Nancy and Tad came out to see them, and Beatrice, oddly enough, drove out several times during the first few months. She said she liked seeing how the other half lived. And once every

165

week or so Lina went to town to lunch with her and hear the gossip of the office.

She kept her little car, and enjoyed it. They had no maid, but the heavy cleaning was done and she found that she had plenty of time on her hands. It wasn't so bad the first summer. They could always jaunt off somewhere evenings in the car, or people came out. Then, too, they began to make acquaintances among the young married people near by. The apartment was in a four-family house, with porches and yards. Jimmy grew friendly with the people downstairs and those next door. Lina, lonely at first, welcomed his gift for making friends, and so it came about that they were asked next door, or downstairs, for bridge and eats, or that they went with other couples to the movies, or drove out into the country for "Dutch" suppers.

It was amusing for a while. It was new. There were even elements of pleasure in it — not having to race off to an office, not coming home in the rush tired and dragged out. They took up golf and played at a public course and found themselves more and more drawn into the life of the community about them.

The days Lina went to town to shop and see Beatrice stimulated her at first because of the newness of her situation and the fact that she was busy at home; she suffered no great nostalgia for the office. She still felt close enough to consider herself a part of it and not an outsider. But little by little, through the things that Beatrice said or did not say, she began to realize that she was, after all, an outsider — a suburban housewife who had once had a job and had it no longer.

By autumn there were changes in the agency. Galleon had left and taken a position in the broadcasting station; Onslow was still on the Coast. Someone else was running the Jelly Joy hour at the agency end and a new girl had come in who was, Beatrice reported, far too pretty to be up to any good; she was doing the Jelly Joy announcements over the air. Lina listened to her and didn't like her at all. When, during a bridge game, she turned on the radio and requested her guests to listen and comment, she was annoyed because they preferred their bridge and thought, if at all, that the woman who made the second of the commercial announcements had a nice voice — "not that I like women on the radio," her partner, the young man from downstairs, informed her.

They accepted her as Jimmy's wife: a good housekeeper, an attractive girl who played a fair game of bridge, drove a car, and was a credit to their little circle. The women thought it a pity that she had no children and said so, asking her intimate questions with the astonishing lack of reticence that distinguishes the confederacy of young married women. This annoyed Lina very much. It was none of their business.

Speaking of business, she had expected them

to be impressed by her past record, but it was evident that they were not. Mrs. Morrison, next door, one flight up, had been secretary to a steel man before her marriage. "And I was glad to get away from the grind! Of course, I missed it at first. It had a certain momentum which carried me on after I stopped. But after Junior arrived . . ."

Mrs. Lenard, downstairs, had never worked and was frankly glad of it. She had been married after her graduation from high school. Her husband managed a chain store in their district and they had three small demanding children. They never had much money, one of the youngsters was always "down" with something, and their mother looked thirty instead of twenty-four, but they were absurdly happy. Mrs. Jackson, next door, ground floor, Had Money. She was the daughter of a wholesaler and she had her own income. She had a car and a son in the sixth grade and dressed almost too well. She'd done a little work, along social service lines, for the fun of it, before she had married. She liked being married a lot better.

Lina saw a great deal of these three women, their respective progeny and husbands. She did not care for children. They irritated her if they were noisy or dirty or fretful. Handsome, well-mannered children were all right, if you didn't have to see too much of them, but she told Jimmy during the following autumn that if something wasn't done to subdue the various

168

roller skating, yowling, teething small fry around her they would have to move despite the good location and the small rent. "Why Bessie Jackson doesn't live somewhere else —" she said — "not that I want her to, I'd miss her, and thank heaven her Bobbie is a decently behaved youngster —"

Jimmy replied shortly that Mrs. Jackson lived on her husband's income except for her car, her frocks, and an occasional luxury. She even liked living on it; moreover, Jackson was going places. He was clever; he had excellent contacts. It wasn't his fault that customers' men were no longer held in the esteem of once-upon-a-time.

Lina had sharp words with the two other women on the subject of noise by day and noise by night. There were periods of coolness between them and when Jimmy returned home from work at such times Lina aired her grievances. He listened, disliking it all very much. He thought their neighbors pleasant young people; he liked them and preferred to live in peace with those about them.

However, these times passed, as they generally do, in this particular class of society — no hair pullings, no threats, and no dragging to court as happens in a lustier and more vital and franker class. And Lina continued to play bridge and go next door for a cup of tea, or to a mending party. She even joined a small women's club to which they all belonged, which was one part charity, eight parts gossip, and one part bridge.

But the talk was always the same, spinach through a masher, and what to do when "they" won't eat, and "My dear, I'm losing all control over Junior," and "Sally said the cutest thing yesterday," and "Yes, Harold insisted that I have a maid but I have had fourteen in eight months and none of them are worth their salt," and "Do you suppose the James Wrights are on the verge of a divorce? I saw her lunching in town the other day with Mr. Thomas, and I happen to know that's his specialty when it comes to the law . . ."

Babies and servants and gossip and how much does so-and-so make and they say she's terribly extravagant. Cooking meals and washing up and dusting and going to a movie. Once in sheer desperation she thought perhaps she'd try her hand at writing. Practically everyone wrote nowadays and she had been a good copy writer in her day and if that wasn't fiction, what was it?

But somehow she couldn't get characters on paper. They wouldn't live and she couldn't "make up" plots, so that phase passed too. And she told Beatrice in November that she was getting fed up.

"It's the same old round. I've tried hard. Jimmy knows I'm trying. But — stupid people and nothing to stimulate you, mentally. Just talk about kids and servant problems and isn't so-and-so too much and isn't someone else living up to every cent of his income. I get so sick of it I could scream."

Beatrice said, after a moment, "Sure. You laugh at it, and I do too, and so do a lot of people. But it's life. Three meals a day and a bed to sleep in and children to worry about and neighborhood gossip, which is a way of relating contemporary history, holding a mirror up to everyday ordinary events. We're not any better, when we have jobs. We talk about the office and about our friends. There isn't much difference. Only you happen to find one amusing, and it flatters your vanity; the other doesn't."

"You make me tired," said Lina, laughing. "You'd hate it; you'd go crazy."

"I would," admitted Beatrice, "but that doesn't prevent me from seeing that it is from such material that the pattern of living is woven. You've been making your living out of appealing to the housewife. You realized, in the agency, how important she is. Just about the most important thing in this or any country. Now that you no longer make your living from her, you despise her — at close quarters."

Lina said, "Don't lecture. Tell me what's going on. Anything happened at the daily showdowns? How's the mogul?"

Beatrice replied briefly. She added, "I won't be able to report to you much longer. I'm quitting the first of the year."

"Beatrice, you're not!" Lina stared at her,

aghast. "Beatrice Harris, I can't imagine you married."

Beatrice smiled, a little wryly. "I can't either," she said, "but I was once, you know. No, I'm not getting married. Funny thing, marriage. The men I'd like to marry never want to marry me. I'm a swell guy and all that. But they're terrified of me. And they don't need my income. Those who do need it would marry me tomorrow, as ever was, but I don't want 'em. No, Lina, I'm leaving the agency and going over to the Thorpe, Wayne outfit — at ten thousand a year to start and a free hand."

"Beatrice, that's marvelous." Lina flushed and her eyes shone, but it was not with wholehearted pleasure. She thought, *If Jimmy hadn't been so stubborn — if I hadn't been such a fool — if I'd hung on, when Beatrice quit I might have had her job.* And she was sick with envy of Beatrice Harris who was entering one of the oldest firms in the country with "ten thousand a year to start and a free hand."

Beatrice said gloomily, "I may be making a mistake. I know our old treadmill like the back of my hand. I know the reactions of every manjack in it. I can see my way around with my eyes shut. I know how much I can get away with and how much I can't get away with. But the Thorpe crowd is different. A little more Sacred Cow, a little more conservative. Thorpe's a holy terror. He's got an international reputation in more ways than one. But in the office he's Strictly

172

Business nowadays. He doesn't mix 'em. And moreover he doesn't like bright young women. Had an experience with one of them some years back which cost him plenty to hush up and since then he ignores the presence of the predatory female when at work. He's discovered that, despite their fame, the agency is a bit on the old-fashioned side and so he's taking me in to try to see if I can pep up things — feminine angle stuff and all that. He doesn't want to. He'll ride me like mad. He's been forced to take me. I'm not as sure of myself as I was." She paused and grinned. She added, "You know, of course, that if you were still in the game I wouldn't be talking like this. I would keep up my back hair and give you the reverse side of the medal."

That night, as they were eating their dinner at a local place, as they always did when Lina had been in town, she told Jimmy about it. She remarked, looking with distaste at a teashop salad, "If I'd stayed —"

Jimmy laughed, a trifle off guard. "You'd have had Beatrice's job, you think?"

"Yes," she said angrily, "why not? You needn't look so smug. I don't think I could walk into it the next minute. But after all, I was the logical candidate."

"What about the women who have been there longer than you?" he reminded her.

"Old dodos, most of them. I wouldn't have been afraid of them. I had something and the bosses knew it, Jimmy."

He said, "So you're sorry you gave it up."

"Why shouldn't I be?"

He shrugged. He said presently, "I've noticed lately that you have taken to rubbing it in. Not directly. But when we're with people. You say things then. Little things. Laughing. But you're not laughing in your mind."

She said urgently, "Jimmy, I *am* trying. But I get so bored. So terribly *bored*."

He stared at her, the red hair redder against the sudden pallor which his tan could not conceal. The waitress stopped at their table and smiled at him. "Was your beef done right, Mr. Hall?" she asked.

Jimmy said, "Fine, thank you." The waitress moved on, her hips somewhat evident, her hand to her platinum hair. The Halls had been coming to the shop ever since they moved out. She liked him. She didn't like the wife. Some might call her pretty. Not she. Too washed out for her taste. What men saw in some women!

He said with an almost pathetic eagerness, "Lina, you don't really mean it, do you? You've the house, you've friends, you can take the car and go places. We had fun this summer, picnics, golf. And it's pleasant to have neighbors. We didn't have them in New York."

She said, with soft violence, "It's sickening. Everyone knows everybody else's business. Babies crying, paper walls. I know when Guy Morrison's had too much to drink — or when —"

174

He broke in, "Perhaps we can find a small house, farther out. You'd like that better. Lina, if you'd let go. With your mind, I mean. Settle down, try to be happy with me, interested in my work. You used to be, when it meant something to you. It doesn't any more. Thousands of women leave business, marry, make homes. They miss the office for a while, that's only natural, but they forget it after a time, and substitute other interests. They take a pride in their homes, they have children."

She said, "For heaven's sake, don't *you* start that! I hear it on all sides. You'd think I'd been married ten years. As if there weren't plenty of time. These smug women make me sick; they're sorry for me, or they're a little shocked. I met one, at Bessie Jackson's just yesterday, who put me through a sort of catechism. I'd never laid eyes on her before. What right had she? She has a couple of grown children herself and says she's 'just living to be a grandmother.' " Lina made a small sound of disgust.

Jimmy laughed. "That is a bit thick, I agree," he said. "Who was she?"

"Oh, someone named Dalton."

"Not Fred Dalton's wife?"

"I think that was her name," said Lina, not interested; "she'd come up from town."

"I've met Dalton," said Jimmy; "played golf with him and Jackson one day. He's in a food brokerage concern. Small, but more successful than most . . ." His voice trailed off; his eyes

175

were remote. He thought, *Lord, I'd like to be on my own, like that. But I can't afford it. Too risky. I've got Lina to think of —*

Lina yawned. She said, "I suppose there's a picture we haven't seen."

"I'm going to have some apple pie," said Jimmy, as the waitress hovered near again; "how about you, Lina?"

"Small cup of black coffee," Lina ordered. She thought, *I won't let myself get fat. I won't eat and eat and eat out of sheer boredom and nothing else to do!* She thought further, and with satisfaction, of her clothes, which were very good indeed. The expensive ones had been bargains, after all, for they would have to last. She couldn't expect Jimmy to buy replicas for her.

Driving home from the movies, they saw that all the lights blazed in the apartment downstairs. A doctor's car which they recognized was in front of the door. Lina sighed, "One of the kids again — croup I suppose; we'll never get any sleep." But Jimmy was out of their car and knocking at the Lenard door. "Is there anything I can do? What's up?" he was demanding.

Lina, behind him, caught a glimpse of young Lenard's white, distraught face, and heard a child screaming. She saw Eva Lenard pass through the living-room, a pan of water in her hands, her face as set as stone.

Lenard said hoarsely, "Thanks, Hall. There's nothing. It's Patsy. She ran away just half an hour ago — in her nightgown — out the open door — in this cold — a car got her, at the turn — Dr. Hawks is here — he's taking her to the hospital —"

"Lina and I'll come in and stay with the other kids," said Jimmy.

"Thanks," said Lenard, "that's decent of you."

It was two o'clock before they returned from the hospital. Lina, worn out, listened to their incoherent outbursts — they were so grateful — yes, concussion, and her right leg fractured — but she'd pull through, they knew she'd pull through — thank you so much for staying.

Upstairs, she undressed wearily. The Lenard youngsters had been hard to handle. She didn't know how. It was Jimmy who did the reassuring and the storytelling, who brought the drinks of water, and sang the silly songs, and even changed the baby.

"Tough," commented Jimmy, unlacing his shoes.

Lina said wildly, "They may think that's living! I think it's hideous. Scared to death half the time — worried — never knowing what will happen next — anxiety, bills. Eva looks twice her age!"

Jimmy said, "Maybe she wouldn't want it any different. I mean, she takes the bad along with the good. That's her job. Any woman's."

"It isn't mine," said Lina. "I know men think that every woman is born with the maternal instinct. Well, I wasn't. It would drive me crazy,

177

having such a responsibility day in and day out. And I'm awkward with children. I don't know what to do or say — they don't arrive with instructions tied to them and a full set of maternal reactions!"

"I know," said Jimmy, "but women learn."

"Well, I don't want to," she said. "I've learned enough tonight. And I don't like children. I'm scared of them."

She began to cry from sheer nervousness; Jimmy went over and took her in his arms.

He said, "Lina, you're wearing yourself out — over nothing. You won't give in; you won't see that you've just exchanged one job for another. I'll compromise as much as I can. We'll get another place, after the first of the year. I might even run to joining the Country Club. Lina, if you'd only try to see it my way."

"I am trying," she wept. Her arms tightened about him, and she pulled him down and kissed him. Her tears were wet on his face. She said, "I will try, Jimmy — I will."

Chapter Twelve:

ON THE ROCKS OF BOREDOM

Before January they moved into a tiny house, in a restricted section. Unfortunately they needed new curtains and other things and the savings account was drawn upon. Jimmy thought, looking ahead to the spring when he would come into his legacy, *I can put it back then and, after all, we are saving. Lina deserves a place she really likes. It was living at pretty close quarters.*

They still saw their first neighbors and there were others with whom they soon became friendly. The new house was minutely perfect and it entranced Lina temporarily. But when Beatrice came out, looked it over, and called it a Doll's House and her Norah, it lost something of its charm. Nancy and Tad, now that they had a guest room, came for a week-end. Nancy said, looking at the all-electric kitchen, "I could die of happiness in a place like this."

"So could I," said Lina; "not from the same cause."

It was no use. She had tried, she was trying, but there were moments when she wanted to throw things and howl. She stopped going to town to lunch with Beatrice. Beatrice irritated her, much as she liked her; she was so confident, so slick, so secure. For she was, she reported, making good with the new firm. They liked her, they'd given her a campaign to handle. She was, she declared, having no trouble at all. It was swell. The best move she'd ever made.

Jimmy wondered. He wondered aloud, to Lina, "I don't think she's as cocksure as she was."

"Oh, but Jimmy, she is. Why, the world's at her feet!"

"I'm not sure. She protests too much. I don't believe it's all plain sailing. She had her own way pretty much before. But I'll bet this is different. Lina, mind if I ask Dalton to dinner? I mean, would you ask Mrs. Dalton? I'd like to know him better. He's a great guy. So are the two younger partners."

The Daltons came and Lina suffered Mrs. Dalton's advice on draperies and conversation which centered about the daughter at Vassar and the son in prep school. Dalton and Jimmy talked shop. They talked Americo and they talked food brokerage. And they talked politics, after dinner, over the bottle of good port Jimmy had brought home. They talked of the labor trouble in the old year, walkouts in the clothing trade, the textile strike in September, the San Francisco matter in July. They talked of cigar makers, of stockyards, and of the longshoremen in New Orleans.

The women drifted upstairs, the men drank more port and smoked cigars, and settled back to enjoy themselves. Dalton said lazily, "Nice little place you've got here. Didn't buy it, did you?"

"No. It's for sale, though. I've been thinking. I'll come into a little money presently. I've thought of it for years as an anchor to windward. I'd like to put some of it in an annuity for Lina. I planned to invest the rest. But with things as they are — I wonder about real estate. In the present depressed market this place could be bought for a song, and it's brand new. The builder never intended renting. . . . Perhaps it would be a wise thing to do. Ground of your own. Something tangible. But then — government bonds . . ."

"Ever think of going into business for yourself?"

"There's only one business I know anything about," said Jimmy, "and I'm in no position to buy Americo."

Dalton smiled. He was a pleasant lean man with graying hair. He said, "I meant my racket."

"I've thought of it, all right. But no one knows better than yourself the risk — and the failures. I can't afford it, for Lina's sake. If I were free . . . but I'm not."

Dalton said slowly, "I understand Perkins, my youngest partner, is retiring. Ill health. He has to live in Arizona. Luckily he has a private income and his wife's well off."

"Lord," said Jimmy sincerely, "I'm sorry to hear about it. I met him only once, but I liked him."

"If," suggested Dalton, "you thought of buying an interest in anything . . ."

Jimmy's heart raced and then almost stopped. He shook his head. "That's swell of you. But you see how I'm fixed? I — I haven't the nerve. That's just about the size of it. Lina gave up a very good job when I became district manager. It was asking a lot of her. I have to make it up to her and the most I can offer her is security. I'm not getting any fortune as you know, but the checks are regular."

"I see," Dalton told him, "but if you did happen to change your mind before Perkins finds anyone else —"

He heard his wife's voice on the stairs. She was saying, "Well, what I always contend about the educational system —"

He grinned slightly and reached for his port. Edna was a good wife, none better, but she was a little wearing. He wondered how Mrs. Hall was standing it — Edna's best clubwoman manner.

"Such people!" said Lina, some time later. She flung herself into a chair and hearkened gratefully to the sound of the Dalton car driving away. "That woman is like a steam roller. He's all right," she conceded carelessly, "if a little subdued, which is to be expected. As for his wife!"

"At least," suggested Jimmy, "she doesn't talk about the things which annoy you. She's a very well-informed woman."

"Too darned well informed, if you ask me," said Lina. "She told me upstairs that being in business robs a woman of her femininity, and when she quits she has difficulty making adjustments. She said it very patronizingly, as if she were sorry for me! What does she know about being in business?"

"Well," said Jimmy, with a feeling of triumph, quite understandable in the situation, "she used to be a statistician with a big life insurance company before she married. She was something of a trail blazer and had a highly paid job for those days."

"For heaven's sake!" said Lina blankly.

He thought, *If I tell her what Dalton offered . . .* What was the use? If she thought it a good gamble he was bound to disagree with her. And if she agreed with him that they couldn't afford the risk — well, where would that get them?

The winter wore on, with snowstorms and sleet and pavements glassy and treacherous with ice. A hard, long season; and Lina found it more trying than the previous year. She read of people "mushing" to parties in Westchester and of a young couple leaving an evening affair at the Ritz, donning snowshoes in the lobby and gaily snowshoeing off down Madison Avenue. Cars were stuck in drifts and people in remote villages died because the doctors could not get to them. Sleighs came out of hiding and replaced motorcars and the poor shivered and hungered and prayed for the weeks to pass.

For some time Lina was shut in. Jimmy managed to reach his office easily enough, but she could not use her car. She was afraid of bad roads, even with chains. She stayed at home and tried to read and found the books dull and stupid; she played the radio until another dance orchestra seemed the final straw. And she thought about New York. She thought of crowds and lighted windows, of the downtown section glowing golden at night, of shops and restaurants, of office buildings. . . .

She grew thin and irritable and quarreled with Jimmy on the least provocation. Once, losing patience, he told her that she was behaving like a child. A little weather wouldn't hurt her. What if it was below zero? She could bundle up and go walking, couldn't she? From her attitude, he remarked, one would think that he had taken her to the wilds of Greenland instead of to a civilized community. She had warmth and food and a pleasant house. She had friends. She had everything essential to living and to happiness.

"Except something to do," she reminded him. "I'm going insane, sitting around all day long."

There were things she could do, and he told her so. She could interest herself in local charities — in underprivileged children — in hospital social service work. Other women did and got a great deal of pleasure out of it.

Lina laughed at him. That was sheer nonsense. She wasn't trained; besides, she didn't like the idea. Volunteer work was absurd. Either your work was good enough to rate pay or it wasn't good enough to serve any purpose.

Bessie Jackson came to see her now and then, and the Lenards and the Morrisons kept up the acquaintance. But she was no longer as attractive to them as she had been. She made no effort. Her nerves were ragged. She was argumentative and, at times, even unpleasant.

Toward the end of February Jimmy asked her, in despair, what the hell she did want?

"I want to go back to work. I'm bored!"

"You're bored," he said, "and it's your own fault. You don't want to go back to work. It's been almost a year —"

"What's a year?"

"Twelve months. You'd find it hard to get back into harness. You'd hate commuting."

"I wouldn't commute," she told him angrily. "We'd move back to the city."

"My work is here," he reminded her quietly.

"Well, then, you could commute," she told him. "Thousands of men do. I tell you, I'm sick and tired of it. I'll find myself cutting out paper dolls presently."

Jimmy knocked out his pipe. The little sound of wood against brass made her wince. He said, "There's no use going over all this again. You're not going back to work and that's final."

She said violently, "You're making a big mistake. I warn you it won't be long before I'm as sick and tired of you as I am of everything else. Mooching around the house all day, with nothing to do but wait for you to come home to dinner! I suppose you think you're Santa Claus, bringing a bit of cheer and a glimpse of the great big outside world to the shut-in, when you do arrive! Well you're not. Same old thing, day in and day out. You arrive and eat and read your paper and listen to the radio and tell me that things are going all right at the office. I can sit around and tat or bite my fingernails. When it isn't snowing or hailing or raining, we can go to a movie, or people drop in for bridge and a highball. It's a wonderful life."

He said, "Life's pretty much what you make it."

"You talk like an editorial," she said crossly. "Of course it is. I could make it interesting and alive, for myself, for both of us, if you weren't so stubborn, so unutterably selfish. I've given your way a fair trial, Jimmy, and I don't like it. You might try my way for a change."

He said, "If you're serious about this, if you're not just talking, permit me to remind you that I *have* tried your way and I didn't like it either." He regarded her for a moment. He laid down his pipe and put his hands to his red hair and ruffled it as he always did in moments of agitation or excitement. "The trouble with you is that you haven't it in you to play square. When you finally decided to keep your promise to me, you did so with reservations. No matter

186

what happened, you weren't going to like it. You were going to suffer — and not in silence. You haven't any guts!"

"You needn't be coarse," she told him coldly; "and now that a year has passed, will you please tell me what you have given me in return for all I sacrificed?"

"Myself," said Jimmy.

Lina shrugged. "I suppose you'll be telling me that I didn't have you before."

"Did you?" he asked, "I don't think so. I know I didn't have you. And haven't now."

"Then you admit it's been a failure!" she said triumphantly.

"I admit that you had willed it to be a failure," he told her slowly, "but I will not admit that it need have been. When we married I thought of it as a partnership — co-operative, mutual, sharing, a sort of give-and-take proposition. You must have learned these rules, in business. Perhaps you even obeyed them, to some extent. I don't see why you can't adjust yourself to a partnership in marriage."

"I don't belong here," she said, "a housewife in the suburbs! I belong in town, in an office. I'm wasted here. Anyone will tell you that. You're just too obstinate to concede it, that's all."

He said, rising, "I'm not going to spend the evening quarreling with you, Lina. Jackson asked me to come over tonight. The Daltons are there. He asked you too but I refused, because I knew what you'd say beforehand. You couldn't be bothered to dress and trek to the Jacksons'. They were not entertaining. You wouldn't make the effort. When Beatrice and any of her merry little pals find the way out here you make it all right. But they haven't felt like hiring dog sleds recently. Personally, I'm delighted, I was fairly fed to the teeth with that gang before we left town."

After he had gone she curled up on the divan and stared into the embers glowing in the fireplace. She thought, *If I get a job, then he can't do anything about it; if I do, I'll make it up to him. He'll see. He's bound to see how much happier I'll be.*

He'd told her often enough that her happiness came first with him. Well, now he could prove it. She went upstairs to look over her clothes. The suit with the beaver. It was in good condition; she had worn it very little. She took down hatboxes, looked into shoeboxes.

Presently she came down again and went to the desk and wrote a note to Mr. Shaw.

A few days later Lina was in town. She went directly to the office of the advertising agency. Everyone greeted her with cheers. "Here's our little housewife back again," they hailed her. "Eating lots of Jelly Joy these days? Lina, you look swell."

Even the harassed office boys, the reception clerk, and the girls at the switchboard seemed glad to see her.

Walking through to Mr. Shaw's office, her heart lifted. This was what she wanted, this was where she belonged. All the activity and the confusion, the excitement, the sense of being part of something big and important. She heard Howard swearing furiously as she passed his half-open door and grinned, wondering what had gone wrong. When she went into Shaw's office her cheeks and eyes were brilliant and she carried her slim person in the hunter's green and beaver like a banner.

"Well," said Shaw cordially, "sit down. I'm certainly glad to see you."

"Tell me the news," she urged him. "If you knew what it's been like, cooped up all winter. . . . I had to see you, and the office again." She smiled at him, intimately, almost caressingly, and Shaw cleared his throat and marveled that he had forgotten how attractive she was. "We've missed you," he told her.

"Not as much as I've missed you," she said. "Tell me about everyone. I know about Beatrice Harris, of course. I see her occasionally."

His slight frown did not escape her. She went on rapidly. "It seems odd without Beatrice, or Mr. Galleon, or George Onslow. How is he, by the way? I've had some very funny postcards from him."

"He's returning," Mr. Shaw told her. He leaned back in his chair and fitted the tips of his fingers precisely together. "He did a very good job on the Coast but we need him here. We're planning a big campaign, on some of the Americo products. Your specialty among them," he added smiling. "And we've the Langborn hat account now."

"That's grand," said Lina.

Shaw cleared his throat again. He said, quite formally, "I hope that your husband is well, and that you are very happy."

Lina's eyes lifted to his for a moment and then dropped. She thought fast. She thought, *If he believes I want to get back just because I'm bored — he's so old-fashioned — no —*

She said, "Yes, Jimmy's fine and we're awfully happy. Of course things haven't been going so well —"

"But I understood he was promoted."

"Yes. He's working hard, making good." She couldn't jeopardize Jimmy's job with Americo; Shaw was in very close touch with the higher-ups in that organization. She hesitated a moment and then said with every evidence of frankness, "You know, Mr. Shaw, I wanted to give up my work, much as it meant to me, because I thought that divided interests are not good and I did want Jimmy to have a real home. But, we've had trouble financially. There were certain investments — you remember the little boom — well, we came out the wrong end of the horn; and then Jimmy had family obligations."

Her tone endowed the orphaned Jimmy with an aged mother, an ailing father, and half a dozen sisters to see through school. Mr. Shaw looked properly sympathetic. His heart warmed toward her. Plucky little thing, good worker too. A flair for copy writing, clever, and with none of the qualities that had irritated him in Beatrice Harris. And Lina was loyal too, which was more than he could say for the Harris minx. He liked Lina's attitude, her willingness to give up her job for her husband's sake, and he suspected, her present willingness to return to it for the same reason. He asked gently, "Were you thinking of coming back to us, Miss Lawrence?"

Her heart pounded and the blood sang in her ears. She said, with timidity, "I didn't dare — hope. But I want to — I feel I should, for so many reasons." She smiled sadly. "It will be a wrench," she said, "to give up the funny little house. I've become pretty much the complete housewife; but do you know, Mr. Shaw, this last year has taught me a lot about housewives. Things you can't ever learn from direct mail campaigns, from questionnaires and house to house calls — even from men in the field. I've had to pinch and scrape, buy and plan as I've never done before. All my energies have been bent on it. I think I've gained a pretty valuable viewpoint." She added, after a pause, "If there were a place for me —"

He said, "I was thinking about that. We haven't replaced Miss Harris. Her work's been split up among a number of people. I realize that when you were with us you were engaged to work on one product only. If you'd like to try your hand, on several? I can't offer you Miss Harris's salary. You understand that. You haven't had the experience, and it took her some time to reach that figure. But I think I can safely say that if you wanted to return to us at your old salary —"

The eyes she raised to his were full of tears. She faltered, twisting her fingers together, small-girl fashion, "If you knew how grateful I am, Mr. Shaw —"

So after a little further conversation, it was arranged. Beginning Monday.

"But commuting?" he asked her, at the door.

"I'll manage till we make other arrangements," she replied. "Jimmy doesn't mind trains. He likes them. Wanted to be a locomotive engineer when he was a youngster."

Alone, Shaw congratulated himself. He had procured a good copy writer in Harris's place, and one who wouldn't cost him her salary and who would turn herself inside out to do the work.

When Jimmy reached home that night, expecting to go to the teashop, he found dinner ready. Festive, that dinner, roses on the table, caviar on crisp crackers and a cocktail in the shaker. "What's it all about?" he asked, astonished and delighted. She was sorry — she had repented of the recent coolness between them, he thought.

Lina wore her prettiest frock, a hostess gown, smoke-gray as her eyes, with a girdle of cherry.

"Going to wash dishes in that?" he asked.

"We'll stack 'em."

"You came back early," he remarked after the cocktails had been disposed of and they were midway through the meal.

"Yes."

"What did you do in town?"

She pushed her plate aside and put her elbows on the table. She rested her chin on her linked hands and looked at him. She said, "Jimmy, you're going to be sore. But you'll get over it. Darling, you *must* get over it. Can't you see I did it for you, to keep our marriage, to keep our love, to —"

"What *are* you talking about?" he asked. The glow imparted by the cocktail was fading. His nerves tightened.

"I went to the agency," she said, "and saw Mr. Shaw. I've my job back. I start Monday."

Jimmy rose to his feet. He upset his glass and the water ran and soaked into the damask. Neither noticed it. He said, "Behind my back. Sly. And all this stage setting. All right, Lina, you've got your job back."

"So what?" she asked evenly, pretense falling from her.

"So you can do without me. That's final. Take your job and leave me. My mind's made up too. God knows you haven't tried to be much of a wife in the past year, but I'm not going back to the other arrangement." He walked around the table and stood looking down at her. "Do I make myself clear?" he asked.

"Perfectly," said Lina. "You tried this Il Duce role before. I was a sap. I chose you. This time I choose the job."

"All right," said Jimmy. "Have it your way. We'll break the lease. I'll take a room at the hotel. Tonight. If you want to see me you'll find me there. But I doubt if you want me."

"No," said Lina, "I don't. You're a selfish, egotistical —" For the first time her voice broke. She screamed at him, jumping up, stamping her foot, "Get out," she cried, "get out — *I never want to see you again!*"

Chapter Thirteen:

LET GEORGE DO IT

Early spring sunlight slanted through the windows of a glorified teashop which served Spanish atmosphere, South American coffee, French cooking, and prices which in any language mean money. There were daffodils on the tables and the waitresses were costumed as female pirates, or perhaps, as they had been selected for their pulchritude, pieces of eight.

Lina looked with distaste at a salad which had been put through a wringer. She pushed the plate away and sighed. "I'm not hungry. I didn't get in till three this morning," she confessed.

Beatrice laughed at her. She was greeting the season in a vernal green suit, collared in seal, and wearing a pancake beret, smart, unbecoming, expensive. She said, "You're looking rather washed out. Freedom isn't agreeing with you. You haven't heard from Jimmy since I saw you last?"

"No," Lina replied, "I haven't —" she drew her fine brows together and the gray eyes darkened — "that is, not since just at first."

"Skip it," said Beatrice. "I know it by heart. Big Brute Goes His Way. The headlines are not unusual. When you are willing to give up your silly notion that woman's place is in the office, you can come home and all will be forgiven. But this time it has to take. No changing your mind after a year."

"I wrote him," said Lina vigorously, "and told him that if he wanted a divorce —"

Beatrice laughed again. "That was a gesture, and you know it. You've no grounds. And the agency isn't paying your salary while you ride a bronco on some Reno ranch. You know that and so does Jimmy. Besides, you don't *want* a divorce, do you?"

"No," admitted Lina faintly, "I suppose I don't."

"All you want," said Beatrice, "is to have your little cake and eat it too. It has been done. Result: indigestion, chronic or acute. You ought to know. You've nibbled."

"He's so damned unfair!" said Lina and smote the table with her little fist. A roll leaped from a butter plate and cascaded to the floor. A female pirate looked pained, picked it up, bore it away.

"That's what you think," said Beatrice; "but let's forget it. I'll bring the new boy friend around to the flat tonight, if you're free."

"I've a dinner date," said Lina, a little self-consciously, "but we'll come back. How about nine-thirty? And who is he?"

"Oh, a pristine find. Rough diamond from the effete East. Very rough. Fun though. And, confidence for confidence, who's the dinner date?"

"Just George Onslow," Lina answered casually.

"Aren't you seeing a good deal of little Georgie?" inquired Beatrice thoughtfully.

Lina shrugged and smiled. She said, "He's been very decent to me."

"No doubt," agreed Beatrice, "but watch your step. Remember the old nursery rhyme about another Georgie who kissed the girls and made them cry? There was a nice tag line about running away too —"

"Don't be absurd," said Lina crossly. "I've known him a long time, after all."

"Yes," said Beatrice, "that's true enough. But your position is different now. In fact, you haven't any position, socially speaking. You are neither wife, widow, divorcee, nor legal separee, if there is such a word. You're neither flesh nor fowl nor that excellent red herring. When you were in the agency prior to your break with Jimmy, George Onslow was attentive and helpful and — careful. George is a big vital he-man, with a wandering eye and an effervescent heart — but he's afraid of husbands. It's a phobia with him. So he plays safe. But now — well, Jimmy isn't at all in evidence and I've no doubt you've informed Mr. Onslow that it's all over but the signing of the papers — haven't you? No, you needn't answer," she said, laughing, for Lina's quick angry color had been evidence enough. "I don't blame you. Bully for our side. A good story is always bettered by embellishments. In any case, you're fair game now and that's that. But I warn you, George isn't a marrying man. When — if — he does marry, it will be a source of great astonishment to him and, I'll bet you a month's salary, a dear little Home Girl with bonds in the bank and a vacuum under her finger wave."

"You're taking a lot of unnecessary trouble," Lina told her coolly. "I can handle my own affairs, Beatrice."

"I'm afraid so," said Beatrice, not too cryptically. " 'Scuse it, pliz. I was only trying to do you a good turn, though heaven knows why; I'm not given to good turns. I must be a sissy. Give me the menu. I could do with a spot of pastry or something." She beckoned the pirate, gave her order, and listened to Lina's stern "Just a demitasse, please," smiling. "How's the work going?" she asked.

"Like a house afire," Lina told her. "Shaw's had me on the carpet twice this past week but to praise, not to condemn."

When they parted, it was to assure each other that they'd meet at nine-thirty. Lina, back at the office, drew circles on a pad, and pondered. She had counted on the evening alone with George, had said, "Let's not dance — let's go back to the apartment and talk." She'd asked the part-time maid to stay in and serve sandwiches and highballs, late; not that she needed a chaperon, but it was as well to be on the safe side. There were some things she wanted

George to straighten out for her, which she wouldn't ask him in the office, and over a dinner table it wasn't possible. Well Beatrice would be late, she always was, and if Lina managed to hurry George a little with dinner, they could be back at the flat at nine.

She had taken a little apartment near Beatrice's. It had been a bargain. Fully and well furnished, it had been sublet for the bare rental by the previous tenants who had been called West. There was a living-room with a dining-alcove, and small bedroom, a tiny kitchen, and a bath. The address was good.

Some day she'd have a larger place, and her own things. She counted on a raise in the autumn. It cost more to live alone than she'd realized and she'd had to have clothes. Onslow took her out a good deal, she went out with Beatrice's crowd, she met other men. That cost plenty. She'd get clear, however, and start to save. Jimmy had sent her personal belongings to Beatrice's, where she stayed while looking for a place to live, together with the rest of her clothes. She had packed in such a fury that she'd left half of them. She assumed that their furniture had been put in storage. She wouldn't ask for a stick of it, not even what was rightfully her own. She'd starve first; not that you can eat furniture, except vicariously. Jimmy had just sent on the things and the one letter; she'd written him, as she'd told Beatrice, but had had no reply. She didn't know where he was or what he was doing and, she told herself, she didn't care.

But she did care. She was often hideously lonely. At first the little flat had been fun. The sense of utter freedom, such as she had not experienced even when she shared a place with Nancy, had been heady and exciting. It was fun to come home when you pleased, to read half or all the night, if you liked, to keep your rooms as you wished them, with no one else's belongings cluttering up your personal neatness. This place was yours, you paid for it, in it you could do as you pleased.

She played at housekeeping, getting her own breakfast and liking it. The maid came in the afternoon to clean and to prepare dinner if Lina was staying home or entertaining. She wasn't at home much. She could usually count on a dinner invitation somewhere. That had appealed to her as having thrift as well as entertainment value until she realized that she had to dress for these occasions and needed, therefore, more clothes than she had planned.

But one grew accustomed to freedom, after a while, and there were evenings when she came in late, and shut the door on laughter and companionship and amusement and snapped on the light and looked about the living-room and felt its utter emptiness. On such evenings she was as afraid and forlorn as a child. The first time it happened she ran to the telephone, called Beatrice, and begged her to come around and spend the night. And when Beatrice said, "I can't, I've people here — throw a nightgown in a bag and come on over yourself," she changed her mind and said, "Skip it. I must be crazy." Later, when Beatrice taxed her with it, she confessed. "I was afraid," she told her, "I don't know why. All of a sudden."

Beatrice had nodded. "You'll get used to it. I was that way once myself."

But she wasn't used to it, not entirely. Fear had worn off somewhat but loneliness remained. There were many nights when she cried herself to sleep, flinging the book which could not hold her interest to the floor and lying there sobbing for self-pity, in the darkness, feeling as ill-treated as it was possible to feel. It was all Jimmy's fault. They could have had such a pleasant, well-run, interesting life — if only he hadn't been so stubborn, so absurdly old-fashioned. What was it that Beatrice had called him? "A reactionary. I imagine most men are," she added, "only they have too much — or too little — sense to conceal it."

Well, whatever he was, he was no longer her own; he could not love her and treat her this way!

Another thing Beatrice had said when she first left Jimmy — she preferred to think that she had left him, not that he had left her — still rankled. "One of these days Jimmy will meet some girl who thinks he is entirely wonderful — and then you'll have your divorce, quicker than it takes to say it, figuratively speaking. For by and large the gals with the home complex and the slippers warming by the fire have it all over the rest of us. I don't fool myself for a minute. What the majority of men want is a wife with the appeal of a kitten, the brain of a housekeeper, the skill of a trained nurse — and the wiles of Cleopatra — minus the executioner and the asp. Five, ten, twenty thousand a year earned by a gal's own fair hands are as nothing beside such attractions. Of course, the modern young man takes the twenty thousand . . . and makes her pay for it. But in his heart he'd far rather earn it himself and dole out the house-keeping money to the Good Little Girl. I've told you this before and I'm telling you again. But this time it has some point. Your Jimmy has tried a spell of marriage with a Busy Busi-nesswoman. Let the right girl come along who knows more about kitchens — not to mention other quarters — than she does about an office, and he'll fall so hard that it won't be funny."

Lina remembered this while she was dressing for dinner with George Onslow. He came, shortly after seven, and she was ready for him. She had made a cocktail and they drank it before going down to the waiting taxi.

"Why don't you ask me up to dinner here, some time?" he inquired.

"I have," she replied, smiling. "Have you forgotten?"

"That was with other people. I meant alone."

Lina looked as severe as was compatible with her particular arrangement of features.

"I don't ask young men to dine with me — alone," she said primly.

Onslow laughed uproariously.

"Lina, you are the limit. You're as sophisticated as if you were born in a broker's wastebasket, with a bottle of Château Yquem in one hand and *The Advertising Handbook* in the other. You've picked up all the chatter in an amazingly short time. But there are other occasions when you turn completely Ladies' Aid and upstate and Mother-says-I-must-be-home-at-ten."

"Hush," said Lina, as they went down in the elevator, "don't waste time crabbing."

"We have all evening," he reminded her.

"No, we haven't."

"But you suggested going back to the apartment," he said, "and why couldn't we have had dinner there in the first place?"

"Beatrice and a new boy friend are coming in after," she said.

"Did you know that when you said we'd spend the evening at home?" he demanded.

"Of course not," she replied, quite truthfully, knowing that he would not believe her. He did not. In the taxi beside her he swore under his breath, then laughed, and put his arm around her.

"You're marvelous," he said sincerely.

"We might," she suggested, "get through dinner early."

Onslow shook his head. He said, "I suppose I'll never understand you and perhaps it's just as well!"

They dined at a small French place on Park Avenue, with excellent food and a subdued orchestra. Lina listened to George's anecdotes of his "term" in the West. She had heard most of them before but she had learned that Mr. Onslow disliked talking business — her business — to a pretty woman at dinner and she had learned to listen, prettily and entrancedly. After coffee, a liqueur and a cigarette, they were ready to go back to the apartment. It was nine o'clock, or a little after, before they reached there.

Maisie, the colored maid, opened the door to them and Onslow raised an eyebrow at her as he gave her his things. He said, when she had disappeared:

"Help within call, eh?"

"Not at all," replied Lina, "I can take care of myself! But I thought we might want something to eat later."

"You mean you knew Beatrice would," said Onslow. "I don't know how she manages. She looks like a slat and eats like a horse!"

Lina sat down on the comfortable divan which went with the apartment and patted it invitingly.

"Come and sit beside me," she said.

"It's a pleasure," said George in the manner of a radio comedian, and sat, very close. He put his arm around her and drew her to him. "How about a friendly little buss?" he inquired.

Lina turned her head so his lips touched her cheek. He said, releasing her, "I don't seem to inspire you with any emotion, Lina."

She touched his hand, smiled faintly at him and said, pathetically, "Please, George —"

"If you say 'Don't spoil things' I'll slap your pretty face," threatened George, irritated.

Lina sighed. She said gently, "I wouldn't say that. I couldn't — because I wouldn't mean it —"

"Lina!"

"But," said Lina hastily, "we have to consider my situation. I'm not free, George."

"You're as free as air," he told her; "that unappreciative young idiot made you so."

"Not actually." She lowered her voice. "I — I have to be very careful. If Jimmy should find out that you — or anyone — were here alone with me   I mean — we know it's all right, but it might not look well — and — neither of us can afford a scandal, George."

Under his ruddy tan Mr. Onslow paled slightly. He had no desire to be found waiting for a streetcar, no matter how desirable the trolley station. This put a rather different light on the matter. He had been led to believe that Jimmy Hall didn't care where his wife went or what she did. He looked at his watch surreptitiously and wished that Beatrice would come. He thought, *Of course, Lina may be exaggerating — but —*

Lina said briskly, "Look, George, I wonder if you'd help me? I didn't want to bother you in the office." She produced, as if by magic, some sheets of copy. She added appealingly, "I've worked like the devil on this. And it isn't right. I haven't been to Mr. Howard; I wanted your opinion first. You're so terribly quick."

George took the copy and found a pencil. After all, if young Mr. Hall walked in, with six detectives, he couldn't find anything out of the way, could he, in an ace copy writer condescending to cast his good eye on the copy produced by a deserving little girl in his office? "Let's see it," he said.

He was still working over it, and had it set to rights, when Beatrice and her rough diamond appeared. The rough diamond was something of a shock, being a polo player, with a giggle, a hard blue eye, and an assortment of fancy cuss words.

Onslow managed to linger a moment when the others were leaving. He asked, his hand on Lina's arm, "Look here . . . aren't we ever going to be alone?"

"George, I've told you —"

She looked wistful and resigned. He said, his breath quickened, "There's always my place."

But she merely smiled at him and shook her head and he went on after the others, a puzzled frown creasing his heavy brows. Was she giving him the runaround? He didn't, he couldn't believe it. She was so incredibly feminine, so gentle, almost docile. The sophistication with which he had taxed her was, he was convinced, a front. Meant nothing. Under the veneer she was a frightened small creature, utterly charming. He hadn't really known her well, he thought, until this bust-up with her husband, who must be a fool. George had liked him well enough, the little he'd seen him, but it only went to show that you couldn't tell by casual acquaintances and appearances. Why, he'd even been brutal to the child. Not that Lina had said it in so many words, but she didn't need words.

No, she wasn't giving him the run-around. She was merely being discreet, as she should be, Onslow concluded. Then another thought struck him amidships, and caused him to fling his cigarette from the taxi window and borrow some of Beatrice's polo player's exotic expressions. She hadn't by any chance fallen for him with the idea of marriage, had she? Was that her reason for discretion?

The thought appalled him. Miss Beatrice Harris had been quite sound in her judgment that he was not a marrying man.

For several weeks he avoided Lina. Not too openly, of course, but she knew it and it alarmed her. She was not on as secure ground with her new assignments as she had been with Jelly Joy. And speaking of Jelly Joy, it was now current rumor in the office that the girl who had taken her place on the copy and on the radio program as well had encountered Harry Galleon at the studio and that they were stepping out, with matrimonial intentions, *just like him,* thought Lina, scornfully, *to be caught on the rebound!*

She needed George Onslow. She realized, after the first month at the agency, that she was not as prepared as she had thought herself. It was one thing to work on a product which you knew backward, but another thing to tackle products almost entirely unknown to you. Onslow was invaluable to her. She thought, *I've been silly, I've frightened him away. There was no reason to do it. After all, I can take care of myself.*

Late in April she met him as he came into the office and stopped him. She did not make any mistakes. She spoke as if they had been seeing each other several times a week, as usual.

"Look here, when am I going to try out the new car?" she asked.

Her own car had been left in storage. Later perhaps she'd take it out. But there seemed no point to it now. And George had bought a roadster, he had told her so, casually, a few days previously.

"Any time," he said, perforce; "you set the date."

"How about a Sunday — in the country? We could come back to supper at the apartment. Maisie won't be there, of course, but if you could manage with cold things?"

"If they aren't too cold," he assured her. "Sunday's a date."

He went back to his office smiling. Of course he'd been wrong. She hadn't been giving him the runaround. She hadn't told him in so many words that she'd missed him, but he felt secure in assuming it. Sunday, he assured himself, was a date.

Chapter Fourteen:

LOSING BATTLE

The last Sunday in April was warm and golden and up in Westchester the bare branches of the trees were lovely as a Japanese etching against the sky and every little leftover rain puddle on the roads was as blue as heaven.

George's new car performed beautifully and some time after one they were lunching out New Rochelle way with a view of the Sound and a salt breeze through the open windows. Lina felt relaxed for the first time in a long while. Her cheeks were faintly flushed with color and she had never looked as pretty. George, drinking his second cocktail, decided that; and told her so. Lina smiled at him.

"You shouldn't," she began, and then broke off, her eyes widening as a party of four entered the room.

"What's up?" asked George curiously, his regard following hers.

"Nothing. Just some people I know," she said, and added crossly, "I *would* run into them here!"

"Not friends of your husband's I trust," he inquired with heavy humor, but Lina nodded gravely.

"We both knew them," she said; "we were neighbors."

Bess Jackson saw her at the same time and waved to her, smiling. Lina returned the greeting and addressed herself to her luncheon. She said thoughtfully. "I wonder if they still see Jimmy? I suppose so."

"What do you care?" George asked her. "Forget him, can't you?"

They lingered over their luncheon and the Jackson party left the room before they did. When, however, Lina went into the dressing-room she found Bess there, before the mirror. She rose and held out her hand to the younger woman.

"I'm glad to see you," she said frankly. "I wondered if I ever would see or hear from you again."

Lina said self-consciously, "I meant to write, Bess — but — it all came about so suddenly — I just — well, you know how things are."

Mrs. Jackson looked at her gravely. She said: "I don't. I haven't asked. We see Jim, of course. I presume you know he's gone into partnership with Fred Dalton?"

"In partnership!" repeated Lina incredulously. "He's left Americo? Why, he couldn't — I mean — how did that happen?"

Mrs. Jackson sat down again and did things to her hair with a little comb. She answered evenly, "I thought you knew. I understand that he's bought an interest, from one of the partners who's retired because of ill health."

"Then," said Lina, "he's no longer in Mount Vernon?"

"No," said Mrs. Jackson, "he's moved to town." She rose and looked at Lina a moment. She said, "I — it isn't any of my business, of course; we've never been intimate enough to warrant interference on my part — but — Jim's a fine person, Lina. And he misses you, terribly."

She put her hand on the girl's shoulder and then went from the room without further word. Lina sat down at the dressing-table. She leaned her elbows on the smooth glass and put her hands to her forehead. She felt sick and shaken, desolate and outraged and angry, in one curious kaleidoscopic surge of emotion. It was as if she had been shaken and the little pieces had fallen, altering the pattern.

Jim. In business. Living in New York. And not a word to her.

When later she went out to an impatient escort she hoped that the cold water had done its work and that he would not notice that her eyes were red.

"What happened to you?" he demanded.

"Oh, I met that woman I saw in the dining-room. We got to gossiping," she said lightly. "Sorry."

They went out and climbed into the car. Lina was very quiet during the first part of the drive. George was not insensitive. He asked, "Your girl friend say anything to upset you?"

"Of course not."

"I take it she dwelt on the late lamented?" he probed further.

"Jimmy's left Americo," said Lina, after a moment, "and bought an interest in a food brokerage."

George whistled. "Bread lines for him," he prophesied; "you were lucky to pull out when you did."

"I'm not so sure — about the bread lines, I mean. I understand the concern is successful."

"A miracle," George declared. "Wonders will never cease. What is the name of the outfit? I know some of 'em."

"Dalton and something," said Lina. "Dalton is the senior partner."

"Say," said George with sudden energy, "they're all right. I do know of them. They've weathered things nicely — handle darned good lines."

Lina said, with energy, "But it's insanity, that's what it is. He used his legacy, of course. I think he's gone crazy. Look here, what's the profit — if any?"

"Seven per cent," replied George promptly. "What do you know about the business anyway?"

"Nothing, just what I've heard Jimmy say."

"All right. Step up to the desk and teacher will expound. A food broker maintains an organization independent of manufacturers. He acts in the capacity of the manufacturer's sales force in a restricted territory. The manufacturer, whom we will call Mr. X, for the sake of confusing you, sells him the products at about seven per cent less than he sells it to the jobber and on this differential he makes his living. He maintains a sales force to call on jobbers and dealers. Naturally he couldn't earn enough to keep him in cigarettes if he worked only for Mr. X, so he takes on P, D, and Q as well, if he's lucky. Most food brokerages handle from five to a dozen different lines. Dalton's outfit handles the limit. And very well too. I shouldn't wonder if the dear departed had bought himself into something worth while."

"But the risk!" Lina exclaimed.

"Sure, why not? But what has he got to lose? He has only himself to keep," George reminded her, "and he can afford to gamble. But let's forget him and the rest of the alphabet; alphabets are a pain in the neck anyway. What say we take some funny roads and maybe lease a spot of tea or something stronger at a wayside hostelry before we trek back to town?"

"All right," said Lina.

It was a lovely afternoon and before they headed back the dusk was falling, smoke-blue. And the evening star was bright above the trees. But Lina was distracted. She had no eyes for beauty or for twilight, or for Riverside Drive as they came into the city, or the lights of the Jersey shore, no eyes for the Park and the glowing windows of the tall hotels, or the lines of yellow blooming lamps along the Avenue.

George had found his afternoon rather hard going and felt that it had been wasted. Hell, there were a hundred girls as pretty and as attractive and far more responsive. Why had he permitted himself to be cajoled into spending a Sunday with a woman whose mind obviously was not upon him? His quips fell flat, his line was slack, and altogether he was so disgruntled that he would have welcomed a chance to escape the evening.

But Lina, when they drew up before the apartment, had a change of heart — or at least a motive. She had treated Onslow shabbily for several hours and knew it. She had no wish to antagonize him. Now she favored him with an intimate and dazzling smile and said, gently, "Don't be peeved at me, George. It was stupid to start worrying about Jimmy. But I'm used to it — it's just a bad habit I find it hard to break. He can take care of himself, of course, and what he does now with his money and time is no concern of mine, is it?"

"That," agreed George, feeling better, "is the proper Scandinavian spirit. Woman, lead me to the eats. I'm starved. That tea and toast business was not so good. I could have done with a highball or two."

"You had one," she reminded him, "and you had to drive. But if Maisie hasn't failed me, we'll find everything ready upstairs."

The little apartment had been swept and garnished. There were fresh roses in a blue bowl and a table laid for two. There were cold cuts and relishes and a salad in the icebox, and cakes and cookies in the breadbox. The coffee was all ready to plug in, once water had been added. And there was a bottle of port.

"This," said George, hugely enjoying himself, "is something like!"

He was in his shirt sleeves in the diminutive kitchen doing things to the salad. Only a man could make a proper dressing, he announced, and the kitchen took on the aspect of a shambles in his search for oil and lemon juice, and a clove of garlic with which to rub the bowl. He had a grand time while Lina was changing her tweeds for a little velvet frock. She tied an apron about her splendor and brought things to the table. George opened the port and muttered something about a dessert wine. But it was all the wine that was available, it was good, it had plenty of authority, and George found himself liking the atmosphere of domesticity which carried with it no shadow of responsibility.

Over supper the talk turned on the new hat account and George, his mouth occupied with cold chicken, grew expansive, gesticulating with a fork.

"Hats!" he said. "Why is it that every man takes another man along when he buys a hat? Because he's scared. Because the average manufacturer makes one type of hat — let's take the felts — in different sizes. They are usually styled for one type of face and they are far from suitable to every type. I've often thought of hats

216

styled to type," he said vaguely. "There's the tall man with the round face, and the tall man with the oval face; the short man with the round face, and the short man with the oval face, and . . . well, it's all a question of depth of crown and width of brim," he concluded.

"George," said Lina, amused, "I believe you've hit on something. What's the catch in it?"

"Expense," admitted George. "Each hat in different colors and different sizes. But it would be a boon — to mankind in general."

Lina refilled his glass. She asked, "Who's going to work on the campaign?"

"I am," said George.

"I'd love to," said Lina wistfully, "it would be fun. Something new."

"Might be arranged," he told her generously. "We're having a conference tomorrow at ten. Sit in with us. I'll speak to Shaw. There's a feminine angle to men's hats, after all. You know how wives kick when a man comes home in a new one. 'Oh, why did you have to buy *that!*' they wail in savage accents. 'You look like the last run of shad.' But if the poor devil sticks to a good old lid in which he feels at ease, they nag him until he gets a new one. They say, 'Do get one like Willie Smith's' — and forget that Mr. Smith is six feet two and has a long oval face, while their poor benighted slave is five feet six with a face as round as an apple. So he looks like hell in Mr. Smith's hat!"

Lina jumped up and got a pencil. Returning, she began drawing faces on the back of an envelope. Pencil strokes for arms and legs and bodies, ovals and rounds for faces, and brims over them. George watched her with amusement. She was excited and animated. She asked, "How much have these mad hatters to spend?"

"Plenty," George replied. "After all, they are top of the heap — except the Overman concern, their biggest rival. They want to put on a splash campaign and we've a year to do it."

"They might," suggested Lina, "take kindly to this."

"Cost 'em a lot," said George, tiring of the subject, "and they have been retrenching during the last few years — as who hasn't? But there's money back of 'em — they needn't worry. If they wanted to play around with Type-Styled Hats they could do it, and more power to them. How about clearing away?"

"I'll do it," said Lina. "Get yourself a cigarette and turn on the radio. I'll be back in a moment."

"We missed Jack Benny!" said George sorrowfully, fiddling with the dials.

Lina put on her apron, cleared the table, and stacked the dishes. When she returned she found George in a subdued mood, squinting with half-shut eyes at his cigarette and listening to soft music. She discarded her working gear and sat down beside him. It was getting late and she was sleepy. Besides, she had a lot to think about. She thought, *I wish to goodness he'd go, but I can't rush him off like this right after supper!*

He put his arm across her shoulders. "Nice, isn't it?" he inquired. "I've had a swell day." He had forgotten his annoyance. He was a very volatile young man.

"So have I," she said, smiling.

"Lina. You're sweet. Look here, I'm crazy about you," said George — and most of the port. "You must have known it. What are we going to do about it?"

Lina's heart misgave and warned her. She answered, after a moment, "What can we do?"

"Lots. Look, does that mean you — ?"

"I do like you," she interrupted swiftly, "a lot. And you've been marvelous to me."

"Forget it," he said uneasily; "liking isn't enough." His clasp moved lower and tightened. He said, "I've kissed you now and then — you always turn the other cheek. Kiss me, Lina, as if you meant it, and of your own accord."

She struggled, slightly. She was frightened. She was in a tough spot and she knew it. She said faintly, "Oh, George, please — I —"

But he had forced her mouth to his own. A shudder of sheer revulsion took her. This wasn't Jimmy. Jimmy alone could arouse her response. She thought incoherently and in terms of ancient advertising — *accept no substitutes.* She had never deceived herself that she would, or could. "No — *no* — *!*"

Abruptly he let her go. After a minute, he said angrily, "You don't have to tell me. You can't go me, at any price, is that it? I'm all right to play around with, to take you out to dinner. . . ." He was furious, he had been hurt where he lived, in his male pride, and, while hell may have no fury like a woman scorned, a man to whom it has been made clear that he revolts a pretty woman is certainly a runner-up. "I'm all right," he added, "to do your dirty work for you at the office —"

"George!" She was white with alarm. "That isn't so! I do like you! I —" she thought frantically; found an excuse, seized up on it, "I mustn't like you more than I do — I — I can't. I'm not free, I haven't any right."

She was very nearly in tears. Mr. Onslow disliked women who wept. He was sentimental and it upset him. He steeled himself against her. He said, rudely:

"Baloney. You could be, if you wanted to — but you don't want to — and what would be the difference if you were?"

"*All* the difference!"

George rose and looked down at her. "I don't believe you," he said. "If you think I'm a sucker — I'm not. But I've a keen idea that you've been playing me for one. Listen, I'll ask you a straight question and you'll give me a straight answer or I'll know the reason why. If you were free — and I asked you to marry me — would you?"

She would have given a good deal to be able

to say yes. But she said, "No," very faintly and then, quickly, "But I —"

"Don't say it. You were going to say you know that I don't want to marry you. Well, I don't, I don't want to marry a businesswoman. I've had my fill of them. Now here's another question. If you were free, and marriage didn't enter into it —"

"George Onslow!"

She was on her feet now in what he imagined was a very good simulation of rage. Perhaps it wasn't all simulation. He never knew; neither did she.

"That's that, then," he told her. "And quite enough, too. Good night. And thanks for a very pleasant evening. I'm going out to get drunk and see if I can keep my fingers crossed. I might have known you were like most women — wanting something for nothing."

"And I," she cried at him, "might have known you were like most men!"

"That," said George from the little hall where he was gathering up his belongings, "is a swell exit line. You ought to put in something about the woman always paying. Take it from me — if she can get out of it, she doesn't. As for men — you can't blame a fellow for trying, can you?" The door slammed.

Lina sat down in a big chair. She thought, dully, *There goes my job.* She thought again, *No, never. I'll get along without him. There's nothing he can do, really . . .*

She emptied ash trays, and opened a window. Presently she closed it again and went into her bedroom. She sat on the edge of the bed for a long time. She had made an enemy and a powerful one. George Onslow could do much to hurt her if he wished; he had considerable influence with Shaw, and even Howard listened to his cocksure opinions. He could do even more. He could, and probably would, refuse to help her from now on. She could never ask him again. Any assistance would now have to be offered of his own free will, and if she knew him at all, it would not be forthcoming.

Well, there were other men. There were other ways. She wasn't licked yet.

What, she stormed at herself, *does he take me for?* She avoided the answer. She knew, and she would rather die than admit to herself he was right. So she sat there and built up a pretty little picture of herself in her mind, one upon which she could look without any discomfort. Nice girl, deserted by unworthy husband, struggles to make a living — and becomes a hunted creature. Why couldn't a man be decent and friendly and accept what was given freely and not demand more? A woman was terribly handicapped. Men had all the breaks. It was a man's world. If Jimmy could see her tonight, humiliated, insulted . . .

But Jimmy was going forth gayly on concerns of his own. He'd probably be ruined, and go begging back to Americo for a job, she thought bitterly. He had no right to risk everything he had. After all, she was still his wife.

The world was against her. She rose, swept three bottles of perfume from the top of the dresser to the floor, and then cast herself upon the bed and wept furiously in an aura of gardenia, sandalwood and mimosa which a seasick whale had preserved for this tragic moment, at some twenty dollars an ounce.

Chapter Fifteen:

HONOR AMONG THIEVES

Lina was afraid. She was afraid because she was ashamed, not of anything she had done, but because she had not been quite clever enough — and she was also angry. Her anger was directed at George Onslow, who was stupid and shallow and selfish. She assured herself that she had wept for a friend she'd never had. For he couldn't have been her friend, ever. And then there was Jimmy — Jimmy, who had given her no choice but to leave him to make her precarious way in a world beset with hostilities for women.

She had no one in whom she could confide. She still liked Beatrice Harris more than any other woman of her acquaintance, but she could not tell her what had happened. Beatrice might not say "I told you so" in so many words; then again, she might. That would be unendurable. It was likewise unendurable to know that Beatrice was cleverer than she.

She had always admitted Beatrice's brains, but not that they were superior to her own. Beatrice had had more experience in business, that was all. When she had had as much, she would be her equal.

It was not without trepidation that she entered the office on Monday morning. She would be bound to see Onslow, at the conference. She had no intention of not attending. He had said that he would speak to Shaw and Howard. He wouldn't now. But she would; and he could not repudiate his own words.

Onslow was not in the office. He did not appear all day, for a very good reason. He had made good his promise — or was it a threat? — and many whiskies and sodas, to say nothing of several brandies — neat — on top of the port, had all but ruined him. He remained in his bachelor quarters ministered to by a faintly amused Japanese servant and by an irritated doctor of medicine. The Japanese had telephoned the office. Mr. Onslow, he stated, was very sorry, please, but he thought he was dying. This information elicited such howls of alternative anxiety and mirth from Howard that Onslow was forced to whisper faintly into the receiver. It was, however, quite true that he feared he was dying — at one moment; the next he feared that he would not die.

Lina passed Howard's open door and halted a moment, listening shamelessly to his final profanity as he replaced the instrument. Then she went in, and looked at him anxiously. "George ill?" she inquired.

"George is ill," he reported gravely, "but I think he'll recover. He must have overestimated his capacity."

Lina said, hurriedly, "About that Langborn account. George promised me he'd speak to

225

you about it — about me, I mean. I'm awfully anxious to try my hand. There's a feminine angle to men's hats, after all," she said, smiling. "Think of all the wives who weep when husbands come home with the wrong hat." She laughed and Howard laughed with her. They had never been close but he had always liked her. Smart youngster. Too bad her marriage hadn't been a go. "Anyway," she went on, "I have an idea — it may be all wet — but —"

"No reason why you shouldn't sit in and be dealt a hand," said Howard tolerantly. "In fifteen minutes. Conference room."

At ten they assembled, Howard, Shaw, to whom matters had been explained by his copy chief, several copy writers, two of the production men, and Lina. There were graphs and charts and maps decked out with colorful pins, there were sales and advertising figures, and all the raw material. The old advertising copy had been procured for study.

Lina sat by and listened. No one noticed her. At the end of almost an hour Howard, swearing freely, looked up and saw her wide gray eyes fixed on his face. He was thirsty and had acquired a headache, from too many cigarettes. He poked a finger at her and inquired belligerently, "Did you say something about feminine angle?"

Lina repeated and amplified it. The tension relaxed; someone laughed. Shaw said indulgently, "Is nothing sacred to the male nowadays, even hats?"

"Did it ever occur to you," asked Lina, as if she had just thought of it, "that a manufacturer might be a jump ahead of his competitor if he styled hats to types?"

"Blond or brunette?" grunted Howard, breaking a pencil point and swearing gently, but Shaw looked up with quickened interest.

"What do you mean by that?" he inquired.

Lina explained. She re-explained. She drew pictures. She said, "Of course, it would be expensive. But — if they were willing to take a chance?"

"By the Lord Harry," exploded Howard, "you may have hit on something!"

Two days later Onslow returned to the office. He went into Howard's sanctum and sat down and looked as he felt. Howard grinned. "While you've been basking in idleness," he reported, "we've been going places." He pushed a sheaf of notes across the desk. "Cast your bloodshot regard on that," he advised.

Onslow looked, and looked again. Then he asked, grimly, "Whose bright idea is this?"

"None other than little Lina's," replied his superior. "And it's a wow. Shaw's been in touch with our clients. He's going to Connecticut to talk things over. It might work. It's new. They can afford it."

The door closed. Onslow had walked out. Howard looked in blank astonishment at the polished panels. *Either he's got amnesia,* he decided, *or the last spree is still hanging over, or else he's sore because he didn't sit in. Well, that wasn't our fault.* He picked up his phone and barked a number into it and, waiting for the connection, forgot all about his ace copy writer. He knew him very well. Moody, incalculable, but invaluable. With half an ear he heard another door bang. He did not know it was Lina's.

"Oh," she said, looking up, "George." She rose from the desk and spoke quickly, her eyes on his hostile face. "I'm sorry you've been ill. I —"

"Skip it," he urged briefly, "I've just been listening to your marvelous idea for Type-Styled Hats."

Lina laughed. It was a creditable performance. She said lightly, "It was half in joke. I never dreamed they'd take it seriously. We were only joking about it the other night, after all."

"We?"

"Well — you said something — I mean it was just the ghost of an idea — and I developed it."

"I'm paid for ideas," he said. "Perhaps it was a joke at the time. A gag. I dunno. Whatever it is now, it isn't that. You get the credit. That's fine."

"Please." She raised her hand briefly in appeal. "I had no intention of claiming any credit."

"Well, don't worry," he told her. "I won't steal it. You're a damned smart girl. I should worry. If it's a flop, well, you can take the credit for that too. Row your own boat, from now on. I'm not in it. The idea doesn't appeal to me. I just stopped in to congratulate you."

The door shut, gently this time. Lina stood there thinking furiously. It was too late to go to Howard and say, "It was George's idea originally." If Onslow decided not to work on the copy, he wouldn't. He was as temperamental as a diva and the agency knew it. He had been with them a long time and on several occasions he had announced that something or other wasn't up his alley. The first time they had forced him, and the result had been nil. The next time they had humored him. They would humor him now. She foresaw, with quickened breath, that this copy might be up to her, in the last analysis; and she was afraid.

Mr. Shaw went to Connecticut. He came back with general orders to go ahead, and the Langborn designers began tearing their scanty hair while some of the more conservative members of the firm put a memo on their pads: *Remember to order red ink.*

Well, there was a year in which to design and manufacture type hats, in which to make surveys and plan strategies, in which to develop new and startling copy.

"Not seeing as much of George, are you?" asked Beatrice carelessly, during a warm, enervating June.

She was sitting beside Lina, in Lina's apartment. There were half a dozen other people there. George Onslow was conspicuous by his absence.

"No," said Lina, "I'm not."

"And why, if Grandma dare ask?"

"Things," said Lina, shrugging, "grew just a little difficult."

"Ah," said Beatrice happily, "so you quit under fire? Funny. Now me, that's when I begin to sit up and take notice. Heard anything from Jim?"

She knew of his change of business. Lina shook her head. "Not a word," she said. Her eyes filled, and without volition. She had thought . . . on their wedding anniversary. But the day passed and had been as other days.

She was working hard. Two of Howard's bright young men were working with her. They were of little help. What ideas they had they kept for their own copy. Howard was pleased with them; not with her. She was, he told her, losing her punch. Perhaps she needed a vacation. She thought, *Beatrice might help?*

Her time was not all occupied with those cursed Type-Styled Hats. There were other wares to be cried in an advertising-conscious world. Sometimes she clicked and sometimes she missed. Her batting average was fair. There was help to be had from Howard and from Shaw. But not all the help she needed. She had not realized before how much she depended on George Onslow.

She saw him in the office every day. He spoke

to her, and that was all. It was bound to be noticed; it was. Even Howard, generally blind as a bat to office undercurrents, twitted her on the coolness between them; there were whispers throughout the staff.

Mary Anderson, the girl who had taken her place, resigned and was duly married to Harry Galleon. The agency rallied and made her a present of very good flat silver. Lina, contributing, felt especially bitter. Why couldn't Galleon have stayed and Onslow left? Galleon had been kind; he had demanded nothing she could not give. She could have worked into the radio end of the agency; she was certain she had a flair for script writing.

She was now at the point where she looked at men's hats instead of their faces and grew to bless the sight of a derby or a topper or an opera hat — at least they didn't remind her of Langborns.

Her car had been driven in from dead storage and was eating its head off in the garage. It was of no use to her. She might as well sell it, she thought dispiritedly. But Beatrice discouraged that.

"You'll be coming out to the shack," she said, "and there's always someone who wants a lift."

She said it over a lunch table. She was looking, Lina thought, rather fine-drawn. The polo player was still in evidence. He had offered marriage and Beatrice was contemplating it. "Except that I hate horses," she said glumly, "and I've no doubt he'd stable them in the house. His sweetest compliment is that I look like a thoroughbred. Such subtle flattery!"

Lina laughed. She thought of George. "Eats like a horse," he'd said of Beatrice. She stopped laughing. She disliked thinking of George. If she believed that she could get another job . . .

"I'm fed up," she said presently. "I mean, same old round. I don't suppose there's an opening for me with your gang?"

"There isn't an opening for a sand flea," said Beatrice. "I understand the depression is over. But in common with a lot of people Messrs. Thorpe and Wayne don't know it. They are firing instead of hiring at the moment."

"They hired you!"

"Yes," said Beatrice, "and up to the moment of going to press they don't regret it."

She wasn't sure, however. She had been easing off lately. She knew it, and unfortunately she was not alone in her knowledge. She had been jacked up once or twice, and none too gently. She could get by on the routine work but when it came to new ideas, fresh angles . . . She was so tired of the word angle that it pained her to meet it in print. The advertising and the motion-picture industry had one thing at least in common, she reflected, they had angles on the brain.

"What's new in your bailiwick?" she inquired negligently.

Lina was looking at a man who had come

into the restaurant. He was a short thin man with a round face and he was wearing a hat with a wide brim. She said, "Look at that hat!"

"Whose? Hers?" said Beatrice. "It's several years old, modified Eugénie. Terrible. Now my Ambrose would love it. It would take a horse to wear it properly."

"I don't mean the woman's, I mean the man's."

"Men's hats are all alike."

"That's the trouble," said Lina, laughing.

"What in the world has come over you?" asked Beatrice, staring. Then she nodded and her narrow eyes almost disappeared. She said, "The Langborn account. I'd forgotten."

"I had some bright ideas along those lines," said Lina modestly.

Beatrice smiled at her. "You often have bright ideas. But maybe these aren't."

Lina looked annoyed. She asked inelegantly, "Sez who?"

"Sez me. I can't imagine anyone having bright ideas when it comes to gents' headgear," said Beatrice, yawning. She looked sleepy and indifferent. She was neither.

Lina had opened her bag and seized a pencil. She took the menu and drew on it. She handed the result across the table. "What do you think of that?" she demanded.

"You are wasted," said Beatrice, "on copy. You should go over to the art department. What's this, Nude Descending the Escalator or

Still Life of Three Wild Ducks and a Mock Orange Tree?"

"Be sensible," begged Lina, "what does it look like to you?"

"I've just told you. Otherwise, I assume you are trying to depict manly faces, some in the best of health, others in the first stages of T.B. I take it the dishpans on top of the domes are meant to represent Langborn's best efforts at haberdashery. By the way, are hats haberdashery?"

Lina was becoming annoyed. She said, twisting her pencil in her fingers, "Don't be funny. Langborn's going to revolutionize the industry."

"Do tell," said Beatrice, putting the menu aside. "Sounds like a Five-Year Plan to me. Or maybe a century plant. Elucidate or shut up. I was never good at riddles."

Lina, her eyes bright and her color brighter, elucidated. When she was all through Beatrice said, negligently, "Dream on, darling. It sounds screwy to me. Or else Langborn has money to burn. And how!"

"But," said Lina flatly, shocked as if by cold water, "don't you think it's an idea — I mean — a really new one?"

"It's new," said Beatrice. "Reminds one of the cigarette lighter Ambrose gave me for my birthday — tastefully set in a dead horse's hoof — They forgot to make glue of it. I mean, it gives a lovely light, if it works. Mostly it doesn't work."

It was no use. Beatrice wouldn't or couldn't be helpful. Lina gave it up as a bad job. She said, "Wait and see. By the way, it's off the record, of course."

"Naturally," yawned Beatrice; "honor among thieves."

As they were leaving Lina exclaimed and turned back.

"Leave your gloves?"

"The menu," said Lina. "I left it there — not that it matters."

"I tore it up," said Beatrice. "I didn't want the management sending strait jackets after you. Good Customer Goes Nuts in Café."

But the folded menu reposed in her flat bag of alligator. Beatrice had a use for it. She knew something which Lina did not know, which was that Thorpe and Wayne had long held the Overman Hat account. She also knew that there was a new partner in Overman's. A youngish gentleman who had come into more money than he knew what to do with, which would furnish Overman's with the sinews of modern war. This gentleman was a distant cousin of the last of the Overmans and his money had come via distilleries. It was going into hats because he had a very special grudge against Overman's chief competitor, the Langborn Company. He and the present Langborn vice-president had attended the same university and Henry Langborn had played a better game of poker. Also he had once smote him in the eye, severely; and by remaining on the stag line during a junior prom had reft Mr. Overman's girl from under his very nose. These are all trivial things but they add up. Mr. Overman did not look like an elephant. But he never forgot.

It would be a year before the Langborn people began their campaign. Meantime, if someone worked fast and furiously?

Beatrice had no scruples. She'd never had any. She liked Lina and she had no illusions about her. Better still, she had no illusions about herself. It was dog-eat-dog in this or any other business, including the business of living, and that was that. She had never pretended loyalty toward anyone or anything except, possibly, herself. Lina would have to learn by trial and error. And if what Beatrice was planning to do, as she waited for Mr. Thorpe to see her that afternoon, were to react unfavorably on Lina, that was too bad but did not concern Beatrice. Lina was getting places by her wits. So was Beatrice, and had been for some time. If she had more wit than Lina, that was Lina's hard luck. Beatrice had never protested to the younger girl that she was to be trusted. On the contrary. She had warned her often enough that she was not to be.

She took the menu from her handbag, studied it, destroyed it and drew some pictures of her own. With the new money in the Overman firm, and with the new chief's well-known proclivity for quick decisions and actions, Overman might have an interesting announcement to make in the autumn.

"Blessed event," murmured Beatrice, smiling slightly. The phone on her desk rang. Mr. Thorpe was free and would see her. She reddened her mouth, combed her thick bangs and adjusted her expression to the one of *brain-cum-charm* which Mr. Thorpe preferred. It was up to her to get him to listen to her. If he wouldn't, well, she could rack her brain for something else. But she hoped she wouldn't be obliged to do that. A painful process.

She took herself and her little pictures into Mr. Thorpe's private office and prepared for battle.

Lina spent the following week-end, and all the week-ends following, at Beatrice's. The first one was pretty bad. She remembered last summer; she remembered this very room and Jimmy in it. She remembered him standing at the window looking out over the lawn and quarreling with her over that silly little Southern girl — what was her name? She'd forgotten and it didn't matter. What mattered was this room and herself in it, alone.

But the week-end and the ones which followed were very gay. There was always an odd man or two to amuse her — some of them very odd indeed, and others quite presentable. There were half-hearted flirtations and flattery and for an hour or so the sense of being brilliant and very desirable. There was sunshine, swimming, everyone piling in the car in bathing suits — there was dancing to a radio, and full moons over the trees, and there was plenty to eat and drink — sometimes a little too much. And there was always Monday morning, back at the office.

The office held less glamour for her than it had. It wasn't merely that she could no longer rely on Onslow's help. It was that perhaps she missed the stimulus of planning, of scheming for that help, missed putting on her little act, missed the triumph when it succeeded. Day after day went by, routine days, with work, some good and some indifferent and some bad. She listened to office politics and squabbles and buck-passing and sometimes took a hand in it and sometimes through sheer inertia did not.

One night, after the opening of a brilliant theatrical season, she went to a play with Beatrice, Ambrose, and one of Beatrice's male admirers in the Thorpe agency. And just as the lights went down Beatrice pinched her arm.

"Third row, center," she hissed, "just coming in."

The curtain rose and Lina, settling back and daring the performance to amuse her, did not look. But she did when the lights went up again at the end of a hilarious act.

Jimmy and a party: the Jacksons; the Daltons; and a tall blond girl whom Lina did not know.

She wore a hooded velvet wrap over her evening gown, and pulled it about her when she rose to make her way with Jimmy to the lobby, for a cigarette. White fur lined the hood and it was very effective. Jimmy looked well. Lina found herself wondering if the studs he was wearing were those she had given him and if the gardenias the girl was wearing had been given her by Jimmy. She blinked her eyes angrily and thanked heaven that her mascara did not run.

"He looks very festive," commented Beatrice. "Isn't that someone I met in Mount Vernon?"

"The Jacksons — and those are the Daltons. He's Jimmy's new partner," said Lina, as carelessly as possible.

"And the girl?"

"I imagine that's their daughter," said Lina; "she looks very young. I think there was one, in college."

"Let's go out and smoke," suggested Beatrice.

"No," said Lina fiercely. "I won't. It's too absurd. Can you imagine him, presenting me — 'By the way, Miss Dalton, this is my wife.' "

"Yes," said Beatrice, "that's why I wanted to go. So I shall. You do as you like. I'm not married to him."

She went, dragging the protesting Ambrose with her. "I've got to see a man about a horse," she informed him sweetly. When she had gone Lina moved a bare shoulder closer to her escort and talked to him wildly about nothing at all. The curtain was up on the second act before Ambrose and Beatrice reappeared, followed a second or so later by Jimmy and the blond girl. Was she mistaken or did he turn and look back after he was reseated?

"Well," she whispered.

"Very," said Beatrice infuriatingly. "Shut up. I wouldn't miss another line of this for anything."

After it was over Lina lost her handkerchief, dropped her evening bag, made a hundred excuses and delayed her friends until she saw Jimmy's party far in advance, moving toward the exit. On her way out, she asked, low, "Did he say anything?"

"He asked how you were."

"Did you tell him I was here?"

"I did."

"And —"

"He said that was nice and he hoped you were enjoying it. You are right. She is Miss Dalton. Very attractive too. Jimmy couldn't keep his eyes off her."

"You're just trying to make me miserable!" said Lina angrily.

"Why should you be?" asked Beatrice. "You left him for good and sufficient reasons, didn't you? Come on, they won't keep a table for us indefinitely."

Well, she had seen him. She had dreaded it, and now it had happened, and he had not looked her way — or had he? — nor spoken. He did not care, he never had cared. That night she wrote and asked him if it would not be better for all concerned if they procured an amicable divorce. She had to look up his office address in the telephone book, and she cried all over the page as she did so.

That was in October. In November, on a Wednesday morning, Lina was summoned to Mr. Shaw's office. She went in smiling, sure of herself and a welcome. She looked especially fresh and attractive, she had had a good night's sleep, she had come prepared to attack her work with fresh vigor.

Mr. Shaw was standing by his desk. He dismissed his secretary and turned to Lina. He was not smiling. On the desk there was an open magazine, a national weekly. It was open at a full-page advertisement of Overman Hats.

"Read that," said Mr. Shaw, "if you haven't already." Lina looked down. She could not believe her eyes.

"Type-Styled Hats —"

"But —" she stammered piteously, "this — I mean —"

"Just what did you mean," inquired Mr. Shaw, "when you presented your idea to a rival agency?"

Chapter Sixteen:

DOG EAT DOG

"But I didn't," cried Lina. "I — Why it was *my* idea, Mr. Shaw. I couldn't —"

Her mouth shook, her eyes were enormous and strained in a face drained of all color. Her bones felt as if they had been turned to water. She was conscious of an actual physical nausea. She thought, *If he'll only give me time — to think — to explain —*

Yet the only explanation was perfectly clear and had been from the moment she set eyes upon the advertisement. Beatrice. Beatrice, hurrying back to her office with a brand-new idea for a prosperous client. *How could she,* thought Lina frantically, *how* could *she?*

"It was not your idea," remarked Mr. Shaw evenly. "Is it possible that you have forgotten?"

She had. She had the type of memory that remembers only what is most convenient. It was a long time since last spring and George Onslow, sitting on the rented divan, talking gayly and casually about men's hats, a long time, even, since the conference at the round table, and George's brief and hostile invasion of her office.

"I saw this last night," said Mr. Shaw, as she stood there not speaking, but looking at him in silence. He steeled himself against that misted regard. "And I called George Onslow and asked him to come over. I showed him this — and discovered that the idea was originally his."

She said hotly, releasing her emotion in what she felt was a justified anger, "That's not true. He did speak of it to me — outside of the office — but in an entirely joking way. He didn't for a minute consider it seriously. I was the one who saw the possibilities and developed them."

"Not altogether," he interrupted; "much was developed in conference. You gave us the bare bones. We all had a hand in building something resembling flesh and blood on the skeleton."

She said, the anger dying, leaving her let down, almost resigned, "If I tell you that I've no idea how this has come about . . . ? It's entirely possible that someone else has thought of the same thing — such things have been known and — or if there was a leak — well, there were other people present at the conference, Mr. Shaw — and —" A brilliant thought took her; she flashed into life, animation. She leaned across the desk, speaking earnestly and swiftly. "Mr. Onslow knew," she said. "He — tell me, Mr. Shaw, didn't he refuse to work on the account?"

"He did," replied Shaw, without a flicker of encouragement.

"Did he give any reason?" demanded Lina earnestly.

"He said, if you insist upon knowing, that the

idea did not appeal to him."

"That all fits in," cried Lina triumphantly. "Why shouldn't he? He — Oh, don't you understand?" she begged, wholly feminine, pleading, twisting her hands together, while the color rose slowly to her temples. "He has a — a personal grudge against me. It isn't possible for me to tell you about it. It was, I prefer to believe, a misunderstanding on his part. I'm alone now," she said with frail dignity, looking as unprotected as possible, "and I'm open, I suppose to certain — oh, never mind. But couldn't he, out of vindictiveness —"

"No!" barked Shaw so loudly that she shrank back, her heart pounding. "No, he couldn't. I know Onslow, I've known him for a good many years. Whatever else he may be, he is an entirely honest and loyal person. I don't know what your quarrel was. I don't want to know. But I do know that Onslow is incapable of selling his organization to a rival agency because of some personal feeling against a woman. And there's no use wasting my time and yours. This account" — he flipped the pages of the magazine with thumb and forefinger — "is handled by Thorpe, Wayne. Beatrice Harris is employed by them. We know that you are friendly with Miss Harris and that you see her frequently. Whether you told her about this inadvertently or deliberately doesn't matter. However, I prefer to believe that yours was not a deliberate disloyalty. In any case,

244

your usefulness in this organization is ended. We cannot afford to employ people who talk too much."

That was all there was to it. No amount of anger, pleading, excuses, even, as an about-face stratagem, apologies, could move him. She was no longer useful. Hence, she must go. She left the office, her face burning and her throat tight and aching with tears. And she left knowing that there would be no job open to her in any other advertising agency. These things get around. She wouldn't have a chance — anywhere —

She wasn't staying the week out. She was quitting, now and at once.

On her way to the office she ran into George Onslow, and was almost in his arms before she realized who he was.

"Hey, steady on," he said, as astonished as she at the collision.

Lina freed herself. "You — *you* — *!*" she said, and the tears rained down her contorted face. She gasped, and almost ran the last few steps to her own office. People turned from desks in the big outer room through which she was forced to pass, to look after her, and whisper among themselves.

Alone, with the door shut, struggling to control herself, she slammed her things together, her breath catching. It wasn't fair. She was being let out, blacklisted, all hope of a career gone because of a man who had wanted more than she could give, who expected an impossible payment for the slight help he had afforded her, and because of a woman who had professed to be her friend and whom she had liked and trusted. Between them they had made her the victim of their treachery and greed.

Onslow went into Shaw's office. He said, without preliminary, "I just ran into Lina — literally — she was crying . . ."

"No doubt," agreed Shaw; "she's been fired."

Onslow looked at him uneasily. He held no brief for Lina, he had no desire to see her, ever again, but he was a good-natured person, and in the main as sentimental as most men. He said, "Look here, she'll be up against it — she won't be able to get another agency job —"

"You're telling me?" inquired Shaw, with extraordinary effect, as he rarely used slang.

Onslow said, hurriedly, "Couldn't you reconsider? Hell, I hate to think I've been in any way responsible —"

"You haven't been," said his superior. "You're a damned fool. Your idea or hers or mine — what does it matter? It was her idea to broadcast it to that unscrupulous little —" Words failed him, or remained unsaid at any rate. "I don't suppose that she did it deliberately. But we can't afford to hire gabby copy writers. I've always said women talked too much! And now," he said gloomily, "we're in a nice spot. I've got to go to Connecticut and talk fast. Things are well under way there. I suppose we'll have to go on with it; it means too much money and work and time thrown away if we don't. But the Langborn people aren't going to be any too pleased. As for you, you'll have to get over your temperamental objections to the account. We'll need the smartest copy we can get and it's up to you to find a new angle and work at it. Don't stand there gawping at me. Sit down. I want to talk to you about it."

Lina, her things assembled, waited until the lunch hour when she could be fairly certain that there would be very few people to witness her departure. Then she left, trim and attractive in her new — unpaid-for — autumn suit. There was no one she knew in the elevator except some clerks who greeted her casually but looked at her with curiosity. But waiting at the elevator door on the ground floor was Onslow.

She would have brushed by him, but he caught her arm and, short of making a public spectacle of herself, she could not wrench away.

"Lina — I've got to talk to you."

"There's nothing to say."

He said, however, his face grave for once, and anxious, "If there's something I can do?"

"Haven't you done enough?" she asked bitterly. "You've lost me my job and any chance of finding another."

"That's very unjust," he told her strongly. "I didn't get you into this mess."

She lifted her scornful eyes to him. She inquired, "Are you sure? After all, you weren't exactly friendly with me."

Onslow flushed a slow, angry red. He said hotly, "Look here, I don't use women's methods. I'll admit I was through being used for your own ends. But I wouldn't lift a finger to see you lose your job. Why should I?"

"I'm sure I don't know," she said indifferently, "and I don't care. You told Shaw that the idea was yours —"

"It was, wasn't it?" he asked reasonably. "I was willing enough to let you claim it. There are more ideas where that came from," he added, recovering himself, "but when he sent for me last night — It didn't alter the situation so far as you were concerned to let him know that —"

"Oh," interrupted Lina, "what's the use? Everyone's looking at us. Let me go!"

Onslow, whose purely benevolent impulse had vanished, said something very like "go and be damned," and then stood there watching her hurry out the ornate door. He took a cigarette from his case and lighted it. That was that. Injured innocence. He shuddered to think of the role he would play in subsequent tales which she'd probably spread among her friends. Then he shrugged. His hands were clean . . . well, fairly clean; clean, at least, so far as this confounded hat business was concerned.

A pretty girl from the art department passed

him and Onslow hailed her: "Hi, Mildred!"

The girl turned, stopped, smiled.

"How about lunch?" asked Onslow gayly, and pulled her unresisting hand through under his arm to his side.

"Okay, big boy," said Mildred happily. "Who could resist you?"

Lina went directly to the Thorpe, Wayne agency. Miss Harris, she was informed, was out to lunch. "Very well," said Lina inexorably, "I'll wait."

She waited until two-thirty in the reception room, feeling faint with hunger and self-pity and anger. Space salesmen came and went or sat down to wait, gabbing through convenient telephones and smoking innumerable cigarettes. The girl at the reception desk yawned and stole a glance at the latest copy of her favorite magazine.

Lina thought with rancor of George Onslow. If Jimmy — Suddenly she was sick for Jimmy, for his broad shoulders and big comforting hands, for the devotion in his regard, the understanding. If Jimmy could see her, sitting there, ignored, flung aside, paying bitterly for her friendship with a woman who had betrayed her. Jimmy'd never liked Beatrice, really — how right he had been. If Jimmy could know why Onslow hated her, turning her employers against her . . .

Beatrice came in unhurriedly and Lina saw her before Beatrice was aware of her presence.

She looked smug, thought Lina, self-satisfied. She had a sparkle in her eyes which spoke of two, perhaps three champagne cocktails — Beatrice liked champagne cocktails — unbearably chorus girl, thought Lina — and her lip rouge was fresh and thick upon her wide mouth. She was disgustingly well dressed, revoltingly chic.

"Well," Beatrice hailed her gayly, "if it isn't Toots. What's on your mind? And what an hour to have anything on your mind!"

But she knew. She had looked just once at Lina and her nerves had tightened and her mind was as alert as it had ever been, champagne cocktails notwithstanding.

"I want to talk to you," said Lina shortly.

"Can't it wait? I'm pretty busy. How about tonight?"

"No," said Lina implacably. "Now."

"All right. Come into my parlor," said Beatrice, and laughter creased her eyelids but was not reflected on her mouth.

When the office door was shut, Beatrice flung off her hat and coat and laid aside her bag. She said hospitably, "Take a pew," and offered an open cigarette case. Lina shook her head and remained standing and cigaretteless.

"I've been fired," she said without preliminary, "and I think you know why."

Beatrice said quickly, "I'm terribly sorry, Lina. But should I know why?"

"Oh, don't," cried Lina, "don't pretend. You

stole my idea — you put it over — got it in ahead — let's not waste words."

"Very well," said Beatrice, "we won't." She drew a long breath of smoke, and it trickled back through her flaring nostrils. "I stole it. So what?"

"So what?" repeated Lina staring. "Is that all you have to say?"

"That's all," agreed Beatrice. "You should have kept your mouth shut. But you didn't. I was growing a little stale. I needed something. You handed it to me on a silver platter. I never asked you to trust me. I've warned you against myself — and most other people — ever since I knew you. You took your chance."

Lina said faintly, "You — admit — ?"

"Naturally. I can't lie out of this one. Neither can you."

Lina said flatly, and in a way pitifully, "But I *liked* you, Beatrice. I thought you liked me."

"I did," said Beatrice, "I do. That has nothing to do with it." She leaned back in her chair and looked at the younger girl with narrowed eyes. "I was in a spot, that's all. I've been working steadily for a long time, and I haven't conserved my energy. As for you, you were riding for a fall. It would have come sooner or later. You used Jimmy to get ahead; when you thought he was no longer useful, you kicked him out. Granted he gave you choice, the result was the same. You used George Onslow, and when he rebelled, you wouldn't come across.

251

Don't look at me like that. I don't have to be told everything. There are some things I can guess accurately enough. You used Harry Galleon — and others. This time, I used you. Is that clear?"

"Perfectly," said Lina, with stiff lips.

Beatrice rose. She said, "Well, good-by and all that. If you were like me you wouldn't let it interfere with an amusing friendship. But you aren't like me. I doubt if we'll be seeing each other again."

Lina threatened shakily, "If I go to Mr. Thorpe —"

"What good will that do you?" asked Beatrice reasonably. "It won't get you your job back. Besides, I've resigned. In a blaze of glory. I'm marrying Ambrose, for better or worse. Probably for worse. But I'm sick of meowing and scratching and biting my way up. I'm not as young as I was. I never had any looks. I'm fed up with everything. Polo ponies at the breakfast table will be a novelty at least."

Lina had turned and without another word was making her way to the door. Beatrice, watching her go, said, "Take my advice and go back to Jimmy. There's a job you might make a success of — if you put your mind to it."

The door closed.

Beatrice ran her hands through her hair. It looked like a Fiji Islander's when she was done. She said aloud, "That's that," and returned to her desk. She was sorry for Lina. But she hadn't an atom of remorse. She was that rare human being, a consistent woman.

Dog-eat-dog. . . .

Lina went back to her rented apartment. She thought, walking around it, while Maisie, helpfully asking no questions, found her milk and the makings of a sandwich, *I can't keep this, of course; or Maisie.*

At six o'clock she was so lonely and so frightened that she called up Nancy. Nancy had planned an evening alone with Tad, but Lina's voice on the wire made her anxious. She invited presently, "Come on up to dinner — yes, right away."

When Tad came home she told him, "Lina's coming."

"Oh, Lord," said Tad, "and I'd hoped for slippers and a pipe. If you think I want to sit around listening to how smart she is — I don't blame Jimmy for clearing out —"

"She's lost her job," said Nancy, "and she's terribly upset. Couldn't you help her, Tad?"

"Me?" said Tad with astonishment. "Well, poor kid," he added, "that's a tough break."

Lina went uptown by subway and bus. She arrived ravenous and with the picture clear in her mind. Her version of how and why she had lost her job swelled the veins on Tad's forehead and brought the tears to Nancy's blue eyes. Tad clenched his fists. It would have given him great satisfaction to have broken Mr. Onslow's neck. As for Beatrice — You didn't go around breaking women's necks — still, boiling in oil would have been a pleasant alternative.

"What are you going to do, Lina?"

"Look for a job. I can go back to being a typist. But Americo won't have a place for me now," said Lina, "not with Shaw running in and out, thick as thieves with the bosses. The agencies are closed to me. But there must be something. I'll give up the flat — luckily it's on a monthly basis — and Maisie must go."

She could have wept for her little apartment with the good address and the deft, incurious Maisie.

"You'll have to live somewhere," said Nancy. "We'd take you in till you found a place, but we haven't room, as you know. There's a woman in the apartment below — she has several bedrooms and rents them to business girls, with or without breakfast. It would do as a stopgap. It isn't the best in the world, but it's cheap and you'd be near us."

A week later Lina was a tenant of the flat below. Mrs. Erickson was a stern-faced but amiable person, and the business girls were of all kinds and classes. It wasn't very pleasant, living in one room, surrounded by strangers, going out for meals, reading want ads, haunting employment agencies. And although winter held off, it was cold and rainy and altogether unpleasant. And unpaid bills followed her.

She ate a good many dinners with Nancy and Tad. It was so much easier, and going out cost money. She offered to pay her share, but Nancy shook her head. "Wait till you get a job," she said. Tad was at first hospitable and sympathetic, but after a couple of weeks he informed his wife that it was getting on his nerves. Night after night he ruined a perfectly good appetite, listening to Lina's recital of her woes, her fruitless search for work, and the indignities to which she found herself subjected.

"It won't be long," Nancy begged. "Honest, Tad, I can't turn her down — she's so pitiful. I'm awfully sorry for her."

"Not as sorry as she is for herself," said Tad. "Well, I hope to God she'll find a job soon."

She found one, in December. She had tried several times to see Harry Galleon at the broadcasting station. When eventually she did see him she was closeted with him for almost an hour. He had received her with a slight confusion of manner which led her to believe that his wife, through friends in the agency, had told him the agency version of the affair. And Lina was shrewd enough to know that to protest too great an innocence was not wise.

"It was my fault," she said, wide, frank eyes on his. "I was a fool."

She touched very lightly on Onslow but Galleon, who knew him well enough and did not like him and remembered perhaps a time when he resented his attentions to Lina, for purely personal reasons, drew his own inferences. And then, as to Beatrice, "I did tell her the setup," said Lina, "but we were close friends. I never dreamed she'd use it for her own purposes."

Galleon said slowly, "I'm sorry, Lina. I'll do my best for you."

A few days later he had done so and Lina had a job in the promotion department at thirty-five dollars a week.

Chapter Seventeen:

"BUSINESS GIRL"

Lina's contact with the amazing and intricate world of broadcasting had been limited to her experience with Harry Galleon on the Jelly Joy programs. It had seemed glamorous, her brief incursion into the new adventure. She'd liked it, the sense of breathlessness which was like a continuous rising of a curtain, the audience, the uniformed trimness of page boys, the glimpses of supersalaried stars signing autographs, commandeering elevators.

Her present position held no such dramatic allurements. She was one of a good many young women who performed a routine job. Promotion with its newspaper releases and its star publicity had, of course, interest and excitement and demanded its quota of creative thinking and planning. But Lina's work had comparatively little to do with that end of it. She saw the manager of the department only seldom and then impersonally; she knew him and all his main associates by name and sight, but to them she was just another young assistant whose specialized knowledge and past experience fitted her for her particular job.

Naturally it was known that Galleon had procured the situation for her, by the well-known pull. It so happened that a vacancy had occurred and Galleon had taken advantage of it. Therefore, in a sense, Lina was an outsider; neither the promotion department nor the personnel had taken the initiative in hiring her. A dozen people in the department could have produced candidates in whom they had a personal interest to fill the vacancy and therefore were not inclined to look upon the successful applicant with favor or friendliness.

If she had ambitions or planned any stratagem through which she might aspire to a more important position with commensurate pay, she would have to cope with her problems herself without help.

Her confreres were too busy with their own jobs and their own ambitions to interest themselves in her. Besides, it wasn't long before it got around that Lina had lost her last job through her own fault. Someone always knows someone else whose third cousin has a friend who is connected with the last place where the newcomer worked. Even if the details of the affair, the contours of the shadow under which Lina had left, were not entirely clear to the gossips, they assumed she had pulled a boner and let it go at that.

She made acquaintances among the girls, lunched with them at counters, but once her work was done no contacts carried over. There were the expected number and variety of men who showed a gleam of interest in her when she encountered them. But none seemed worth while; most of them were hard-working young-sters on small salaries, and without the prestige and possibilities of her superiors — whom she did not see at all. She did her work halfheart-edly, therefore, and when it was done, she went back uptown to the apartment. Sometimes she stayed downtown and had something to eat and went to a movie. Not often. Now and then Nancy and Tad took her to a neighborhood house and they sat through the early show. Nancy and Tad enjoyed the neighborhood houses; they liked the crowds on Bank or Sweepstakes or Screeno nights; they played Screeno and the other games for all they were worth and once, when Nancy won five dollars and went up on the stage to receive it, they dragged Lina — furiously bored — to a German restaurant afterward for beer and sandwiches in celebration.

Living in the same building with Nancy and Tad, she saw them frequently, although she did not "run up" for dinner as often. Nancy had at-tempted to apologize for not inviting her as fre-quently as formerly. It had been embarrassing for them both. Obviously it was impossible for Nancy to repeat the words of her lord and master: "Tell her she's a little blond chiseler and we're not taking non-paying guests. Gosh, Nancy, I don't mind having her now and then, I'm not inhuman, but I don't want to fall over her every time I come home. I don't begrudge the extra ten cents it costs to feed her either —

but I feel that she should pay me ten times that ten cents to listen to her eternal complaining."

Tad was doing pretty well. Things had picked up for him in recent months. Lina, knowing this, asked Nancy, "Why don't you get out of here — find a bigger place, downtown? You can afford it."

Nancy shook her head. "Nothing doing," she said firmly; "we prefer to operate on a surplus."

"But that's nonsense. What's the use of slaving, never having anything, just to acquire a little balance? You're young, you're entitled to a good time."

"I'm having it," declared Nancy. "I'm not losing weight, worse luck. I don't think you get our setup, Lina. Just because Tad's making double what he did when we got married there's no excuse to blow it in on a good address and a couple more rooms. We feel *safe* this way. And if you think cooking and cleaning for two people is slavery, well —" She shrugged her plump shoulders and laughed tolerantly.

"You forgot the washing," said Lina. "You'll ruin your hands, you'll lose your looks. It isn't fair to Tad. Just because you married him doesn't mean you don't have to work to keep him."

Nancy flushed. She said impulsively, "You're a swell one to talk!" Then as Lina's eyes filled, she added quickly, "I'm sorry, Lina, I didn't mean it. But you don't understand. I never won any beauty prizes. Tad thinks I'm all right. I don't go around in curl-papers and cold cream and if I have put on a couple of pounds I'm not ballooning and sagging in the wrong spots as yet. We want to save, not live up to our income. We want a place on the Island, and a couple of kids. We're not thinking just of ourselves. We're doing pretty swell and we intend to do sweller!"

Lina shuddered briefly. She had an instant sharp mental picture of the next decade for Nancy and Tad. A white frame house with a picket fence or something semi-detached and bastard-Gothic; scooters in the hall, roller skates on the front steps, and a pram under a mosquito net in the yard. She heard the whistle of the commuters' train and visualized the things the furnace could think up to do in winter, and freezing pipes. There'd be baby clothes drying in the bathroom, and perhaps a slatternly girl to help in the kitchen and some day a small, cheap car and eventually a larger house and a less slatternly maid and the Country Club — and at Christmas a community carol-sing.

Measles and mumps and whooping cough, repair bills for humans and for houses — neighbors' bridge parties, whipped cream and sandwiches, and rose bugs on the six bushes!

Well, everyone to her own taste. Nancy's wasn't Lina's.

There was a short silence. Then Nancy said, "And I send out the flat work and Tad's shirts.

261

If you think it's hard to wash underwear and table linen with an electric washer, you're nuts!"

She looked at her friend across an immense gulf. Then she asked, "And you don't hear a word from Jim?"

"No," said Lina, setting her lips, "I don't."

"Look," said Nancy uneasily, "if he knew you were in a spot — I mean, when you were pulling down a hundred a week you can't blame him for thinking you could get along. But it's different now. If he knew, he'd help. It wouldn't be like him *not* to help, Lina."

"A lot you know what he's like," said Lina bitterly. "And I'd starve in the gutter before I'd ask him for a cent. After all, I have some pride!"

"Seems an uncomfortable price to pay for it," commented Nancy mildly.

She told Tad of the conversation afterward and he laughed loud and long, "I can see her in the gutter," he announced. "And how! Don't pay any attention to her, Nancy, and for heaven's sake stop worrying about her! If she fell in a sewer she'd come out with a string of pearls around her neck and four government bonds in her left hand! She'd run into some poor sap who'd stake her. That baby can take care of herself — with the help of a couple of other fellows."

But Lina was not taking care of herself. She was by nature a fighter and a good one, even if the Marquis of Queensberry didn't interest her. She fought by her own rules and in her own way. And in her present job there seemed nothing to fight for, no one with whom to fight, and no one whom she might enlist in her battles. She'd fought her way up from a typist's position in Americo, she'd fought her way out of the Americo concern into the agency, and now she was stranded in what seemed to her a stagnant backwater with no outlet and no oars.

She expected to be alone at Christmas. Nancy and Tad had gone to Jersey again and there was no one who'd ask her to go out. She thought of other holidays, of Onslow, obsequious head waiters, of Beatrice and her gang. And she thought of Jimmy, bringing home a tree.

Well, it was only one day, thank heaven, and she'd sleep late, go to a movie, fill in the time somehow. But she hated the lights on the trees and red wreaths at glowing windows. Sentimental, stupid, commercial! Good times in the world and none of them for her. She could have wept for self-pity, and did so frequently.

But late Christmas morning the telephone rang in the hall and Mrs. Erickson, heavy-eyed from her Christmas Eve celebration, came to the door to wish Lina a perfunctory Merry Christmas and to inform her that she was wanted on the phone.

Lina scrambled into robe and slippers and went, shivering in a draft and too sleepy to be very curious. "Hello," she said, and heard Stella Jarvis's voice on the wire. "Merry Christmas," she said. "Lina, how are you?"

She had not laid eyes on Stella since leaving the agency. She had not said good-by nor written nor phoned. By now she had all but forgotten her. She said, considerably astonished, "Stella — how sweet of you —"

Her voice broke perceptibly, and Stella said swiftly, "Look, Lina, I wondered — if you aren't doing anything — would you like to come over to a pick-up supper tonight?"

"I'd love to," said Lina; "what time?"

She hung up and went back to her bedroom. She thought, *Sorry for me, I suppose. I've half a mind to call it off.* But no, perhaps through Stella she could learn several things: the office attitude, possibly, and Harry Galleon's. She had not seen Galleon since procuring the job.

She went to an early movie, ate her Christmas dinner in a small restaurant, and returned home, to wait for the bathroom to be free. She took her time in the tub and Mrs. Erickson rapped more than once on the door, announcing that other people had use for hot water. Lina did not hurry. She set her hair, manicured her finger nails, dressed carefully, and with the full knowledge of her extravagance took a taxi to Stella's.

There was a slight constraint in Stella's pleasant manner when she greeted her, which was dictated, Lina was shrewd enough to realize, from her former knowledge of the other woman, by embarrassment rather than hostility. They went into the living-room and looked at the tree and the presents and Lina inquired for Mrs. Jarvis. "I did so want to send her a plant, this holiday," she said, not having so much as thought of it until now, "but frankly, Stella, I can't afford it. I didn't send cards either, I've been too absurdly depressed. But I'll snap out of it," she promised, with her best, brave smile.

Stella said warmly, "It was sweet of you to think of Mother. I'll tell her. She came to the table for midday dinner — we had a few people in — but I put her to bed several hours ago. She isn't up to prolonged excitement."

"How did you get my telephone number?" asked Lina.

"Through Harry. He got it from your office."

"I see. I'm awfully grateful to him," Lina told her; "his was the one helping hand. I haven't seen him again. Of course, he's awfully busy, and — well, you know what a barn that place is. I never even run into him in the elevators."

"I expected him here today," said Stella, "with Mary. You didn't get to know her very well, did you? She's a dear person. But she's ill — a heavy cold — and they stayed home." She indicated unwrapped parcels under the tree. "I should have sent them down, but I hoped till the last minute they'd come."

Later they ate cold turkey, cranberry sauce

and a salad, and drank some sherry. Lina said, picking at a piece of breast, "It was nice of you to ask me, Stella. Pretty desolate — just a room —"

Stella said quickly, "Tell me about it."

"There's nothing to tell. I've a hall bedroom in an apartment — there are several other girls there. I don't know any of them really. Our landlady is the comic-strip type but decent enough. I've friends in the building. Nancy and Tad — Oh, you met them at — at the apartment last Christmas, didn't you?" asked Lina, and looked away quickly. Stella saw her wince and was terribly sorry for her — warm-hearted, sentimental Stella, who had been so shocked at Lina's defection, yet who had tried to make excuses for her.

"It's nice for you, having them near," she said lamely.

"Yes. They've been sweet. But, of course," Lina added, "they have their own circle and life. Nancy used to be my best friend; we shared a place together before — before I married. But it's different now; it's bound to be. I don't expect anything else."

Stella had a vision of Lina, alone in a hall bedroom, listening to sounds of revelry which meant her callous, indifferent friends were amusing themselves without her. Not that she said anything against them. She was too loyal. That was why Stella couldn't understand what had happened at the agency.

She said, with difficulty, "Lina, I thought perhaps I'd hear from you after you left —"

"Why should you?" asked Lina with some spirit. "I waited to see if any of my friends would communicate with me. None did. I — frankly I wasn't risking a rebuff, Stella. I couldn't endure that; it would have been the last straw. If people wanted me to drop out quietly, well, I'd drop and not bother them. I know the office version of what happened and I assume most people believe it."

"What did happen?" asked Stella, and offered her a cigarette.

Lina took one and smoked silently for a moment. Then she said, "I don't expect you to believe me, but —"

Her version, this time. The same facts, softened, colored. Stella's eyes grew enormous. She said with vigor, "I never liked Beatrice Harris, and as for George Onslow — I've no use for him either."

Neither had Lina — now.

Stella, always a champion of lost causes, was full of ideas: she'd go to Mr. Harcourt personally, and to the others. It was all horribly unjust, and if Lina had only come to her . . .

"Don't," begged Lina, "please, you'd only make matters worse. I feel in a way that Harry got me this job only because he was sorry for me, not because he believed a word I said. There's only one thing you can do for me, Stella, and that's set things straight with him.

He's such a dear — and I hate to think he helped me against his better judgment."

"I'm sure," began Stella, "that he did nothing of the kind." The doorbell rang and she excused herself to answer it, as the maid had gone home after dinner. A moment later Lina heard a man's voice in the hall and her heart leaped. She stubbed out her cigarette and waited. She heard Galleon talking as he came down the hall. "Yes, much better — her mother's with her — she insisted on my coming just to say how sorry she was — and to bring —"

He was at the door now, Stella, smiling, beside him. "Hello, Harry," said Lina gravely, "and a Merry Christmas."

Her luck was holding, her marvelous luck which never wholly ran out. He had cared for her once; he might again. Oh, she knew that he was in love with the girl he had married on the rebound, but men are creatures of habit: the nerves habituate themselves, they remember and are electrified, the pulse remembers and is quickened. Harry Galleon would remember once she had the opportunity to remind him. That other time, sitting in his office, surrounded by pomp, circumstance, a beggar, a penitent, it hadn't been possible. Now perhaps it would be. She'd make haste slowly, she'd be cautious, and sooner or later it would mean a transfer to a better position, one in which she could climb.

"Lina!" he said, pleasantly astonished. "I'm glad to see you."

She said, "I look for you over at the cata-combs. But I never see you."

It was said deftly and without reproach. Promptly he reproached himself. He said, accepting a chair and a cigarette and a glass of sherry, but refusing the plate Stella offered, "I've meant to look you up — thought we'd have lunch — but I've been so infernally busy. It's a madhouse, you know."

"I'm getting to know," she said, "although I'm not employed in the violent wards. I sometimes wish I were."

"Like your job?"

"It's swell," she said contentedly. "I'm learning a lot."

He couldn't stay long, he told them. They sat there talking and it was natural that when he rose to go he made the offer, "May I see you home?"

"It's awfully out of your way."

"Not at all. I've my car outside. By the way, what happened to yours?"

"I sold it," she said cheerfully; "one has to eat."

On the way uptown she talked to him of his wife.

"I'm so sorry I didn't get to know her better," she said. "Everyone liked her so much — and she's the *prettiest* thing, Harry. I'd like to see her again — unless —" She hesitated, let it go unsaid.

"Nonsense," he said shortly, understanding, he believed, perfectly. "After she's well — she scared me nearly to death, by the way — you must come have dinner with us."

So far so good. The rest of the time she sketched her present situation lightly and with laughter. The implications were plain enough. Galleon could smell cabbage and fishballs; he could see the other business girls, shabby or tawdry, distinctly inferior; he could see the hall bedroom. He said awkwardly, "I wish I had something better to offer."

"But, of course, you couldn't," she cried; "don't be silly. And I can manage beautifully. I've done it before on less. It was just that I'd grown used to extravagance, I hadn't saved — and now I've got to scrimp to get out of debt. Once I do, everything will be fine. I can't believe I haven't a future," she said wistfully.

"Lina, don't misunderstand me, but if I can help — tide you over . . ."

He was remembering now. She was close to him, there in the car. His heart was Mary's and his whole devotion, but he remembered.

She was clever enough to refuse, gratefully, prettily. The offer made, the refusal uttered, her position was consolidated. He thought, *She's a brave kid; that husband of hers should be horsewhipped.* Lina smiled in the darkness. Now and then she could read thoughts. Why not? They were in her own handwriting.

She was still smiling when she let herself into the apartment. It was eleven o'clock and Mrs. Erickson was entertaining. She reserved her parlor for that purpose, and her business girls could do their entertaining on park benches. She was a respectable woman; no male callers were permitted in the bedrooms.

"Oh, Miss Lawrence," called Mrs. Erickson.

She came into the hall, a little more genial than usual. She said, "I was waiting to hear you come in. Your friend from upstairs she was just down a few minutes ago. She wants to see you immediately. Very important," she said.

"Oh," said Lina blankly. She wondered if Tad was ill, if there had been an accident. For half a moment she played with the idea of not receiving the summons. "Damn Erickson anyway; she never takes phone calls or messages!"

She dismissed the thought, left the apartment, and ascended to Nancy's. Miss Lawrence. She'd almost forgotten she'd ever been anything else.

She pressed Nancy's bell and waited. The door opened and Nancy drew her into the small dark hall. She whispered, urgently, "Lina, if you don't want to see him, I'll tell him you didn't come home. We ran into him in Jersey — there was a to-do at the club and we went over after dinner with Tad's sister. He was there, with some people. I couldn't help telling him about everything — he made me. So he came back with us."

"What on earth are you talking about?"

"He's waiting in the living-room," said Nancy, breathless. "I know how it is at Erickson's. Tad and I'll go to bed — you'll be alone —"

Without a word Lina brushed past her and opened the door of the living-room. A stocky young man with red hair rose from the couch and Tad fled precipitately. Lina didn't see him go, nor Nancy follow. She stood there staring. *"Jimmy!"* she exclaimed, and burst into tears.

Chapter Eighteen:

TO US — FOREVER

She saw his hands go out to her, but turned her streaming eyes away from him and stumbled to the couch and put her head down on the arm. She had shed a good many tears during the past months but they were as nothing to this cleansing flood. To a dispassionate onlooker it would seem that she wept as a woman does who feels her life is ended, and as a child does as it enters life. Yet Lina herself felt nothing save the necessity for escape, for refuge in tears. She cried from reaction, for self-pity, from a sense of bitter injustice and unhappiness. Nor were the tears histrionic, although it was quite possible that she was not unaware of their probable effect.

Jimmy was close to her now, his arms about her; he was terrified, almost beside himself. He kept imploring her to stop, to look at him; he warned, "You'll make yourself ill!" He said, "I'll call Nancy."

"No," whispered Lina. She made a tremendous effort, groped for her handkerchief, clutched the small sodden piece of linen in her hand. Jimmy took it from her and substituted his own. She blew her straight little nose, mopped her eyes, caught her breath, as a child does, and said finally, "I must look like nothing on earth."

Her eyes were swollen and red, the delicate make-up was streaked on her cheeks, and her lipstick had smeared. Her hair was any which way. She looked very plain and Jimmy had never loved her more. He thought painfully, *She's thin — she hasn't been getting enough to eat,* and the belief hurt him past endurance.

"Lina, why didn't you let me know?"

"Know what?" she said, drawing away from him, gradually getting herself under control. "That I'd lost my job?"

He answered self-consciously, "I already knew that."

"I suppose you know why too," she said, after a minute.

He looked at her almost humbly. He said, "There were rumors — they don't signify, Lina. I didn't hear about it till you took the other position — through Galleon —"

The humility was quite gone. She said, "Oh, I see. That information was garbled like the rest, I suppose. Well, Harry Galleon helped me when no one else was willing, after I'd been kicked out through no real fault of my own."

He said, "I know. Nancy told me all about it. I ran into her and Tad in Jersey — I was there with friends — I didn't dream — I thought you were all right."

"I'm quite all right," she said sturdily.

"But you aren't," he contradicted. "When Nancy told me the real facts, I — I could have killed myself for not making you see me sooner.

You see, things came to me in a pretty round-about way, at first. Lina, when you left the agency, why didn't you — ?"

"Come crawling?" she interrupted scornfully. "And ask you to take me back, because I was a failure, because things hadn't broken right for me? Do you think I'm crazy?"

He smiled slightly, for the first time. "Sometimes," he answered, "I do. I know *I* am. Crazy about you, crazy without you. Lina, I've missed you so much. Is it possible you haven't missed me at all?"

She felt her throat thicken again. She said, with difficulty, and with perfect sincerity, "I've missed you horribly, Jimmy."

"Then, why . . . ?"

"You know why. If I wouldn't stay with you when I was successful, I certainly wouldn't when I wasn't."

She had forgotten that it was not she who wouldn't stay. He forgot too, for the moment. He said, looking at her with such pity and love and longing that the shallows of her curious heart were stirred:

"You've had a tough time, you poor kid. You aren't much bigger than a minute."

"I'm all right," she said again; "you needn't worry about me."

"But I do. I've spent a lot of time worrying about you. Then I saw you in the theater that night. You looked — pretty much on the up and up. I told myself, *You needn't worry about her, she's on the crest.* But I couldn't help it, Lina."

She said slowly, "It was pretty bad at first. Not just losing the job — but the way in which it was lost. Oh, I was at fault, in a way; I was a fool, I thought I could trust my friends. I couldn't. Not Beatrice — not — Never mind that."

"I know about him too," said Jimmy. "Nancy told me. If I ever lay my hinds on him —"

"What good would that do?" she inquired reasonably. "Be sensible, Jimmy. It's over and done with. I got myself into it, it was my fault. I thought some men were decent, motiveless — that's how much of an idiot I was — and some men are decent. Harry Galleon is."

"I suppose so," said Jimmy without enthusiasm. He had heard about Galleon from Nancy; and Nancy had hastened to assure him that Galleon was newly and happily married. But it didn't seem possible to Jimmy, who loved her, that any man could be indifferent to, or impersonal toward, his wife.

She said, "I hated the job at first. Not just the fact that there wasn't any money in it. I'd had so darned much fun in the other. I liked it, it had a future, it was up my alley. But this — assembling material for other people to work from, sometimes being permitted to do a rough draft myself but not creating anything really worth while, not seeing any future in it — until recently."

"What do you mean, until recently?" he asked her.

"Just that. I believe now that I can work up in this. I didn't see it at first, I was too disgusted, too unhappy, perhaps just plain dumb. But now — well, I don't know — It may mean a long time, but the job isn't the dead-end street I thought it."

He thought, in dismay, *The job again, any job.*

When he had heard that Lina had left the agency, under unfavorable circumstances, his first reaction had been, *She'll come back to me.* But at the same time he learned of her new position. He had made careful inquiries, very guarded, in the right places and what he elicited had not disheartened him. She'd never stick it, she'd tire very soon of working at something which held no glamour and no future, and her altered financial position would make a difference to her. Sooner or later she would seek him out. Or would she? He knew something of her pride, her fighting spirit, and he was no longer sure that she loved him. After all, he had made the ultimate decision. Had he given her her way she would still be with him.

His first impulse had been to find her. He was sure he could find her, through Nancy; or, failing Nancy, the broadcasting company. He had earlier, shortly after his first knowledge of Lina's dismissal, called up Beatrice. And Beatrice had enlightened him in part. She had concluded by saying that she had no idea where

Lina was, and that she did not expect to see her again.

"You see, Jimmy, men may become implacable enemies over a woman or a race horse or three spades redoubled, or two up on the last eighteen. But when it comes to business enmity — well, that's another thing. They meet at the club and they get drunk together. You've seen lawyers in court calling each other every permissible name and impugning each other's honesty, integrity, and moral character, and you've seen 'em go out to lunch arm in arm. But it isn't like that with women. I'm off Lina's list, and that's that. But what's to prevent you from drinking a cocktail with me, one day? Come on up and see me, some time," drawled Miss Harris, laughing. After which invitation she had added gravely, "I wouldn't worry about Lina. She'll get along."

He thought, as the days went on and Lina made no move toward reconciliation, *The first advance will have to come from her.* And he thought further, *But I don't want it that way; I don't want her to come back to me because she has no other place to go, because it's the lesser of two evils.* Yet he knew that she could come back on any terms.

Now he said, "Lina, I don't know if you know I've left Americo and am in partnership."

"I heard about it," she broke in. "With Mr. Dalton." She tipped her head on one side and looked at him, half smiling. "Miss Dalton's

278

very pretty," she commented after a moment.

He made an impatient gesture. He said, "Never mind all that. It's a good business, and a successful one. We've — I'm not making any fortune, but I'll always make a living, a better one than I've ever made before. Lina, if you think you could be happy with me — ?"

She said quickly, "You know how I feel. I haven't changed. Losing the good job didn't change me. I'm not — a housewife. I suppose," she added with rare honesty, "I'm not a wife at all."

He asked, almost dazzled by the inspiration that had come to him, "Suppose I offer you a job?"

"A job!"

She looked at him, her eyes wide and astonished. He thought, *That's it. Why didn't I think of it before? I've talked about it to Dalton, about hiring someone to do the work, and I never thought of Lina. But, of course, she could do it, she could do it marvelously.*

He said, "I don't suppose you know much about a food brokerage —"

"I know a good deal," she said swiftly, and was back once more in a fast, sleek roadster, riding along the Westchester roads in springtime with George Onslow. "You and your seven per cent!" she added carelessly.

"Well, it mounts up," he answered briefly, impressed by her alertness, and pausing to think, *She wouldn't have bothered to find out if she hadn't cared — a little.* "And here's where you come in. I — we have to be completely posted on the advertising done by our manufacturers and we have to see to it that that advertising is brought to the attention of the jobbers and dealers. This end of the business has been handled by me, with some help from the rest of the staff. But it could be done better by someone who gave it his — or her — entire attention. I talked to Dalton about it not long ago. We decided to hire someone. How about it, Lina? Would you take the job with us? We couldn't pay you a great deal more than you are getting now — at first — but I promise you that there's a future in it — our future. Think it over."

She said breathlessly, "You're just making a place for me."

"No, I was perfectly honest when I said that for some time we've considered getting help. Lina, it would be a partnership. You'd be working, not for me, not for Dalton, but for *us*. For our future, together, because, of course, you know there's a string to it — we'd have to be together — always."

She asked slowly, "I'd have full charge of that end of it?"

"Of course, once you had learned the ropes."

Her eyes were shining now, and her lips curved to a smile. She said, "I expect you'd be a slave driver."

"Then you will, Lina, you will?"

"I don't know," she told him slowly. "Yes,

perhaps. Jimmy, I do see possibilities and if I could work out my own ideas."

"You could," he promised quickly. He put his arm about her and drew her to him. She made no resistance. He asked, very gravely, "But the other partnership, Lina?"

She loved him, she had always loved him. She even liked him. He was the only man she had ever known who could arouse any emotion in her, any depth of affection. He was the only man who had ever compelled physical response as well — for emotion and physical response are not necessarily the same thing. All this long time, before her marriage, after her marriage, during the separation, she had been aware of her love for him. It was the only authentic thing in her, besides her ambition. But she had been aware of it as a weakness in herself, and considered herself as superior to him, of herself as the pace setter, the leader, the dominant factor in their relationship.

She thought suddenly of Galleon. Tonight had laid the groundwork for a contact there which might prove of real assistance to her. But this assistance would be harder to win than before; she would have to use other methods, be very cautious. It would be a long way up. Here was something, ready-made, something in which she could interest herself, something through which she could benefit not merely as a wage earner but as — her boss's wife.

She began to cry again, not with distortion,

not with devastating and humiliating results but gently, almost serenely. She turned in his arms and laid her wet cheek against his own. Now that she had won — for, was it not a triumph, had she not, in the last analysis, conquered, and forced him to a compromise? She could afford to be tender, afford to let him see how happy she was.

"I do love you so much," she told him, "and I've been so lonely. I — when I saw you tonight — You needn't have offered me the job, Jimmy. I would have come back — jobless — no matter what I said."

That, too, she could afford. She could give him back his self-respect, permit him to believe that, after all, he had triumphed, whether he'd known it or not, and that the white flag had not been necessary. For now she was not dealing with a husband but with an employer. And there are certain things which it is as well for employers to believe.

And now, watching the eagerness invade his eyes, and then vanish as if, having learned his lesson, he doubted, she remembered another time when he had doubted her and when she had dispelled that doubt. She remembered how she had dispelled it and in what manner, far from distasteful to her. And she went limp in his arms, sighing, with closed eyes, the lids shining with tears. It was not tenderness which she inspired but a response in which, more often than not, tenderness plays no part. And she was perfectly aware that victory would not be difficult, for in addition to his desire, and her own, there was another enemy to conquer. Memory. Memory and its running mate, habit — the senses remembering, the pulse attuned to a familiar tempo.

She whispered, "If you knew how I'd wanted you!" And it was true! Was true. Truth is a strong weapon, stronger than lies.

For a long time he did not reply. This was not the occasion for words. But when, at last, remembering Tad and Nancy, he held her away from him and looked at the bright color in her cheeks, the radiance of her eyes, the soft tremulousness of her mouth, he said strongly, "You little wretch!"

"But," she said warningly, "you can't go back on your word now. *Let* me work with you, Jimmy. I'd love it. We'd be so much closer together; we'd have such grand times. It would be different — you'll see how different. You won't mind it; you'll like it too. That is," she added, "unless you get tired of seeing me around."

"Twenty-four hours a day's too short," he said, "after what I've been through. I'll never make up for lost time."

He was perfectly happy. If he had given her her way, it was now his way. He had never been sure of her, now he would be. She would be working with him, for him. And he would always cherish his belief that, had he not offered to take her into this new partnership, she would have come back to him because she loved him and wanted him and because she had learned that, after all, their life together counted most.

He got up and pulled her to her feet. "Get your duds on."

"But, Jimmy!"

"Get your duds on," he repeated firmly, "and pack yourself a bag. We'll send for the rest of your things tomorrow. I've a funny little flat in the village. It will do till we find something better. At the moment I'm starved. We're going out and eat."

"Jimmy Hall, it's after midnight."

"Antonio's will be open. There's a back room that's open till almost morning. They'll let us in!"

"But Mrs. Erickson —"

"Who the hell is she?"

"My landlady downstairs. She'll be terribly suspicious. After all, she doesn't know I'm married — and the rent's due Friday."

"I'll take care of all that," he said grandly.

"I have to work tomorrow, Jimmy."

"Okay," said Jimmy, "you'll work, and you'll resign. That's all there is to it. You have a better position. Where's this Erickson female?"

"Floor below, 6-C," Lina answered. "What are you going to do? I have to speak to Nancy."

"Speak away. I'll go down and interview the old battle-ax."

He caught up his coat and hat and ran from the room. The door slammed. Lina went to Nancy's bedroom and knocked and in a moment Nancy poked her head out. Beyond her Lina caught a glimpse of Tad, tousled among the bedclothes, and very wide awake.

"Nancy!"

Nancy, in metal curlers under a net, advanced into the living-room with caution and shut the door.

"Jim gone?" she asked, disappointed. She and Tad had listened shamelessly — to sobs and to the sound of voices. Tad had said, "I wish to God they'd make it up — or something. I want to go to sleep. I will go to sleep. Wake me if he beats her up. I'll go out and help him."

"Yes. No. He's downstairs, talking to Erickson. Nancy, I'm so happy."

"Then you have made it up?"

"Yes," said Lina, "we've made it up."

"You're going back to him?"

"Yes," said Lina, and added enigmatically, "he's found me a job. Nancy, I'm so grateful to you."

When she had gone away Nancy returned to Tad, who was sitting up in bed eying her with severity.

"Now what?"

"I dunno," responded Nancy, bewildered, "she says she's going back to him and that he's found her a job."

"Well," said Tad, with feeling, "the poor sap. Come on to bed, for Pete's sake, and let me get some sleep."

Lina found Jimmy and Mrs. Erickson holding converse in the parlor, the guests having departed. Mrs. Erickson was superb in cerise flannel and curlpapers. Apparently Jimmy had charmed her, for she beamed upon Lina, as she paused beside them, and protested how sorry she was to lose her. She had a little trouble remembering that Miss Lawrence was suddenly Mrs. Hall, but all in all the encounter proved amiable enough.

Lina, washing her face, cramming things in a little bag, powdering, rouging, running a comb through her hair, decided that Jimmy must have paid at least two weeks' rent — in lieu of notice.

Presently she was ready and, shutting the door of the hall bedroom for the last time, came out to where Jimmy was waiting. She shook hands with her landlady. "Thank you so much," she said. "We'll send for the things tomorrow."

"That will be quite all right," said Mrs. Erickson with a deadly refinement. She looked at them, misty-eyed, still genial after the evening's libations. "Such a nice young couple," she murmured. "I always thought there was a little mystery." She shook her finger at Lina and looked like an elderly and very arch horse. "I hope you'll be very happy — this time," said Mrs. Erickson.

It had snowed slightly earlier in the day. Now it was snowing hard as they came out of the apartment house. Thick and soft and white it lay on the pavements and from almost all windows wreaths gleamed green and red in the lights. As they drove downtown in the taxi Lina looked out at the lighted trees outside of the churches and exclaimed softly, with pleasure.

They took Fifth Avenue and saw the great tree at Rockefeller Center glowing from stand to lofty top. And Lina said, her hand in Jimmy's, "I never wished you a Merry Christmas."

"Tomorrow," said Jimmy, "I'll buy you a present."

"I won't be able to do much, this year," she reminded him; "perhaps with my new job —"

"You've given me my present," he said contentedly.

Antonio's was still open. It was just the same. Smoke rising to the low ceilings, impossible murals, the fat waiter beaming. "For so longa time we have not see you —"

"This," said Jimmy devoutly, "is a celebration as is a celebration!"

He ordered champagne. The bubbles rose in the hollow stem and broke delicately. Lina raised her glass.

"To Us," she said, "to our partnership — forever."

"Forever," said Jimmy.

He drank, his ardent regard holding her own. He saw in her eyes such promise of happiness, of understanding, of comradeship that he was dizzy with it, as no wine could make him dizzy. She would have come back on any terms, and of her own accord. He felt soothed and at peace and entirely magnanimous. He told himself, *But it's better this way, she'll be happier.* He had nothing to fear, any more. She loved him, she was his, even during office hours he would be able to tell himself that.

He no longer thought of the job as the bait by which he had lured her. He thought of it as secondary, as a gift, a sop, something thrown in gratis, perhaps a reward — a bright and shining reward, as trivial as a diamond bracelet snapped about a surrendered wrist.

Lina drank her champagne and drew a deep breath. She was, perhaps for the first time, completely happy. She had her own way, and Jimmy wasn't aware of it. He'd never be aware of it. She was aware of a slight contempt that, after all, that way had been so easily won. But — men were such fools . . . they laid themselves wide open. You loved them and tricked them and cheated them — and made them happy.

"To you," she said, drinking to him. To her husband.

But not to her husband alone. To someone more important, someone whom she must keep in good countenance, with whom she must co-operate, in whom she had a definite interest divorced from their intimate relation, someone who could help her, who could further her career, heighten her sense of superiority, whom she must interest and amuse and who would keep her ego occupied.

Her boss.

28.95

LT FIC
Baldwin, Faith.
Men are such fools.